OPERATION: BELOW

BY WILLIAM MEIKLE

SEVEREDPRESS

OPERATION: BELOW

WWW.SEVEREDPRESS.COM

ISBN: 978-1-923165-49-6

-1-

Wiggo was surprised to get called up to the colonel's office just after breakfast on a cold, clear morning in Lossiemouth, but even more surprised to enter the room and find Captain Banks behind the big desk. The room was colder than the colonel kept it, and even had one of the windows open.

"A breath of fresh air is it, Cap?" Wiggo asked as Banks motioned him to a chair.

"The old man's got some compassionate leave," Banks said. "His missus is on her last legs in hospice care. And what with my gammy leg playing up, they've put me on desk duty for a month. Not exactly a promotion, not in my mind. More of a penance."

Wiggo sat down and waited for Banks to speak, not knowing whether what was coming was going to be good or bad for him, or for the squad. It must have shown in his face, for Banks laughed.

"Dinna fret, lad. It's no' a bollocking."

Banks shuffled some papers.

"It disnae seem that long ago that we first met when you were falling arse over tit out of yon contraption in Antarctica. But look at you now. In case you havnae noticed, you've been doing better than all right recently. And somebody else has been keeping tabs on you too. You're up for promotion to Staff Sergeant," he said. "If it was just up to me it'd be automatic, but the brass wants to see you think on your feet for yourself first. So we've got a wee job to be done. Right up our street too."

He read from the papers in front of him, as if familiarizing himself with the details.

"There's a cave system on the German border with Austria, a big deep bugger that swallows the unwary and untrained. And it seems there's something down there that's decided it wants to play up top. Local farmers are losing livestock, villagers are up in arms, cops are baffled; same as it ever was. You ken the drill."

"Aye," Wiggo said wearily. "What kind of beastie is it this time?"

"That's what they're trying to find out. And word of our experience has spread. They've asked for some help; in a purely advisory role. You're going over low-key; sidearms only and even that's pushing it, but dress for the cold as I hear it's bitter over there right now. Take Wilko and Mac, and it's your squad. There's a plane getting prepped as we speak,

2

wheels up at midday. Here's your orders. Your contact details at the other end are in there."

Banks pushed a folder over the desk.

"I wish I was coming with you but it's a cushy number. I don't think there's anything here to fuck up," Banks said with a grin. "But, Wiggo… don't fuck up."

Wiggo briefed the other two over a coffee in the mess twenty minutes later.

"So, another hand-holding op," Wilkins said. "Just like Yukatan."

"Aye," Wiggo said sourly. "And look how that clusterfuck turned out. Ye ken already that things are never simple when we're involved, so we do this the way the Cap would have done it; by the book and by the numbers. At least the beer and tucker should be to our liking."

Kitting up was a simple process of checking out the handguns and clips and getting themselves dressed for winter. They all went for the same look; stout boots, military issue thick trousers, woolen sweaters and dark worsted jackets with deep pockets and high collars, and black woolen caps that could be pulled down over the ears. Apart from that each of them only had a small backpack containing shaving gear, toothpaste, soap and a change of underwear and undershirts. The only other things Wiggo carried were his papers, his stock of smokes and his lighter, with the handgun on his hip and the spare clips on a belt at his waist. Wiggo laughed as he looked around at the three of them, like peas in a pod.

"Smart but casual," he said. "But nobody's ever going to mistake us for tourists. Maybe that's for the best."

"Any clue as to what we might be up against, Sarge?" Mac asked.

"Not a Scooby, son," Wiggo replied, and patted the folder Banks had given him. "But I havnae read this yet. If there's anything scary in here, I'll let you know."

Their plane was waiting for them on the tarmac bang on schedule and ten minutes later they took off into a clear blue sky. Wiggo got the lads settled with coffees then turned to the papers he'd been given. As the captain said, his orders on their own were simple enough, basically boiling down to 'Don't fuck up.'

Another piece of paper was a photo and phone number of his contact, a stern looking German copper by the name of Kaminski.

The rest of the paperwork was a weird mish-mash of things. The first that caught his eye was a re-drawing of an ancient map. Salzburg was up in the top left corner but the rest was a depiction of someone's journey from there along a river and then down into the bowels of the mountains. There was a translation of some old Latin side-text, that told of a Teutonic knight, Lamprecht, his travels from the Holy Land, his flight from the Pope, and his descent into the dark carrying treasure to be hidden. Wiggo couldn't at the moment see anything of value in that or how it pertained to the job at hand, so turned his attention to the next page; a translated police statement from a patron of *Die Hirtenruhe,* a local inn on the mountainside.

"It was just after closing time that we saw it. Pale and white, crawling on its belly, almost snake-like but thick in girth, like a beer barrel with six legs, a long neck and an even longer tail. It hissed at me, sounding more like a cat than anything else, and reared up, as if meaning to attack. I wasn't having any of that, so I kicked it, hard, where I thought its stomach might be, and it scuttled off, away up the hill towards the caves. It was only later that I heard about the calves being taken, and realized I had probably seen the cause. I swear this is true; I hadn't been drinking… well, not enough to be seeing beasts of legend in any case. But I saw it; it was a wyrm from olden times all right, I'd swear on any bible you'd give me."

There was another report, a cold, clear description of the carnage wrought on a pen of cattle that was all the more disturbing for the complete lack of emotion in it. A picture of that site showed Wiggo's contact arguing with a young woman just outside the cattle pen, but there was no context as to what that conversation might be about so he discarded that too. There were several color photos of what was left of the cattle. It wasn't much, but whatever had got at them it had been a vicious bugger, that much was clear. He put the photos aside and checked the rest of the papers.

There was little of note aside from police speculation as to the cause. The captain had been right there too; the local cops were indeed baffled. The squad was going to be dropping in almost blind.

"Same as it ever was," Wiggo muttered to himself, closed the folder, leaned back and closed his eyes.

He was asleep a minute later.

A sleek black SUV waited for them on the runway at Salzburg. It took them away, with no border formalities required, heading south under what was now a heavily overcast sky that promised a dump of snow later. The driver was a dour taciturn chap, who spoke English but proved to be immune to Wiggo's charms. The near hour-long trip took place mostly in silence with the lads in the back and Wiggo up front hanging his cigarettes out the window between puffs.

The driver dropped them off in the parking area in front of an imposing mountain inn that loomed, almost mountainous in itself, on the side of the hill. Wiggo guessed that there might normally be a spectacular view, but everything was shrouded in mist under lowering clouds and flakes of snow drifted down from higher up the slopes, promising much more to come.

"Herr Kaminski will meet you in the foyer in an hour," the driver said, the first words he'd spoken since leaving the airport, and there were no more. He got back in the car and drove off, leaving the three men alone.

"They're really rolling out the red carpet this time, lads," Wiggo said. "Let's check in and get some scran; may as well make use of the expense account while we can."

They were expected at reception and check-in once again went without formalities. Wiggo was assigned a single room at the rear of the hotel high in what might at one time have been the rafters, but any view was even more occluded by mist now, and the snow was falling more heavily.

He met the two lads in the bar area downstairs, and allowed them all a pint of very fine lager each and had a burger that was nearly as big as his head. He was on the point of finishing it off when a young woman approached them at a brisk walk across the bar. She looked familiar, and it only took a second for him to recognize her from the photograph he'd seen on the plane, the one where she'd been arguing with the local copper.

"Here comes trouble," he muttered to himself as she walked directly up to him and put out a hand.

"Sergeant Wiggins? Of the secret Scottish S-Squad? You're the monster hunters, right? We need to talk."

"I doubt that very much, miss," Wiggins replied. "You've got me mistaken for somebody else."

Before Wiggo could turn away she had whipped out her phone and set a video running.

"So this isn't you in the Yukatan a few months back?" she said.

The sound of gunfire was tinny and far off, but the picture was clear enough. It was taken from the back, and showed a soldier, kneeling in the broken fuselage of a plane, firing out at almost-human things that swarmed on an airfield beyond. When the figure turned side-on to reload, Wiggins' features were clearly visible.

"Bloody engineers have to document everything, don't they," Wiggo muttered.

"Yes, they do," she replied. "And the ones in London in the sewers got you on screen too on that job. Do you want to see that? Or I have some footage from a ferry on Orkney somewhere on this thing... I particularly enjoyed the colorful swearing on that one."

"No thanks, lass. You're right. I was there. I've seen it already. But you've certainly done your homework. Not that it's going to get you anywhere, mind. What is it that you want from me?"

"I've been working on the problem here. I heard you'd been called in. But Kaminski isn't going to let you near the caves; you're in his territory, treading on his toes, even if you don't know it yet."

"That's good, because I have no intention of annoying the man. He's got enough on his plate already and we didn't come here to piss in anybody's chips."

"But you will," she replied. "After I tell you what I know."

"You will be telling these men nothing," a clipped voice spoke at Wiggo's back. He didn't have to turn to know it must be Kaminski; he sounded just like he looked in the photo, maybe even more dour and stern. "I warned you not to approach them."

"And I told you I'd talk to whoever the hell I want to talk to," she replied.

Kaminski switched to German. The ensuing conversation was too fast for Wiggo's limited skills to follow but he caught the gist; she was warned off, not for the first time, but was told it would be the last, if she knew what was good for her. The woman turned to leave, but not before one parting word to Wiggins.

"You're going to want to talk to me. Trust me on this."

She was hustled out, none too gently, by a burly copper.

"She seems nice," Wiggo said, turning his attention to Kaminski.

"Please ignore her. She is… how do you say?" He made a turning motion at the side of his head with his forefinger, and smiled thinly. Wiggo already didn't like him much as the German continued. "I suppose you will be wanting to see the scene?"

"Wanting to? Not really. Needing to? Yes. That is if you want our advice?"

Kaminski showed Wiggo his palms.

"I have been asked by my superiors to cooperate. Here I am, cooperating. Let us visit the scene, before the snow covers it."

As luck would have it the 'crime' scene was in walkable distance from the inn, some eight hundred yards up the hill. It was snowing heavier now, big heavy flakes the size of your thumb which were starting to lay a carpet on the flanks of the hill. There was just enough visibility for Wiggo to note that the cattle pen lay another hundred yards or so below an obvious cave entrance on the hillside, one that was cordoned off with police tape.

As for the cattle pen itself, there was little to see that the photos hadn't shown him. Something vicious had got in among the stock, and had made one hell of a mess while feasting.

"Bear, possibly?" Wiggo said.

"That was my thought too," Kaminski said, grudgingly. "Although there have been no bears in this area for a very long time. However, I have trackers out in the woods at the moment. They have found nothing yet."

Wiggo motioned up the hill.

"And the cave?"

"I have it sealed, merely a precaution though. It has been empty for decades, centuries even. Nothing can live down in those depths. Nothing large enough to do this damage in any case."

Wiggo's experience told him that such sweeping generalizations usually came back to bite you on the arse, but this German copper didn't look like the kind of man used to taking advice, so he held his peace and checked the perimeter of the scene. At least the man was efficient; he had armed guards posted, he said he had his trackers out in the woods… and the attack certainly looked like something an enraged bear was perfectly capable of. Short of mounting an expedition down into the cave system Wiggo didn't see anything he wouldn't have done himself.

He was about to tell Kaminski exactly that when matters took a turn; a four wheel drive arrived along a rutted track from the south. There was something strapped to the hood and as it got closer Wiggo saw it was indeed a bear, but this didn't look like anything capable of the carnage in the pen. This was an old, tired, somewhat mangy thing, and where its mouth gaped open in death it showed broken, rotted teeth. This animal had surely been near death even before the four burly locals with shotguns had blasted the fuck out of it.

It wasn't stopping the men celebrating as if they'd won a medal though, and Kaminski was now busy pumping their hands with obvious glee. Wiggo considered airing his opinions, but the Cap's words echoed in his head.

Don't fuck up.

He kept his mouth shut while Kaminski glad-handed the hunters, then came over towards where the three squad members stood.

"It looks like you have made the trip for nothing," the German said. "We have our perpetrator, and my work here is finished. But thank you for coming. I will have a car at your disposal again in the morning to take you back to the airport."

And that, it seemed, was that. Kaminski wasted no more time on pleasantries and was already walking away.

"Well, that's just fucking marvelous, isn't it?" Wiggo muttered. If the brass were after something to confirm his promotion prospects, this didn't look like it was going to get the job done.

He turned back to the others.

"Well, looks like we've got a free night, lads. Last one back to the bar gets the beers in."

-2-

They were on their second beer and thinking about a third when the woman arrived at Wiggo's side.

"I've been wondering when you'd show," he said. "Beer?"

"Yes, please," she said. "And I'd have come sooner, but I had to wait till Kaminski went back to Salzburg."

"What are you, lass? Reporter?"

"No. Researcher… it's how I know about you. But, more importantly for our purposes here, I'm a local. I've got inside knowledge that Kaminski chose to ignore. I'm hoping you'll listen."

"I have beer, I'm relaxed… you've come at the perfect time. Park your bum and talk to me. I promise to listen."

"I'll make it quick," she said. A beer arrived for her and she necked half of it down before continuing. Just as he'd immediately taken against Kaminski earlier, Wiggo already liked her. The three men leaned closer as she spoke.

"I'll make it quick, as there's something you need to see that'll prove my point," she began. "A hundred years ago my great, great grandfather, and three of your countrymen, went down into the caves here. Your men were looking for treasure. What they found was pain and death, for one of them at least. The other three, after many adventures, and on two separate trips, went down deep. To cut a long story short, there is indeed treasure down there, but it is guarded. There is, to put a modern word on an old thing, an ecosystem in these caves, and a wide variety of animals inhabiting them, some harmless, others less so."

"And one of them has been coming up to play? Is that what you're saying?"

"At least one. Maybe several," she replied. "The stories have been passed down through my family over these many years. There are wyrms in the deep. And maybe not so deep."

"And what do you want from us?" Wiggo asked.

"Kaminski is an idiot."

"Obviously. And?"

"And his superiors will need proof before they take anything I say seriously. I want your help to get that proof."

"Proof? What kind of proof?"

"It's best if I show you," she said. "Will you come? It's not far."

Wiggo looked at his beer, thought about what the Cap had said, then looked up into the woman's eyes. Her need was plain to see. He sighed deeply.

"Sorry, Cap," he muttered, then looked at Mac and Wilkins.

"Get yer troosers on, lads. We're going to help a damsel in distress. Same as it ever was."

He finally got her name on the way out to the parking area.

"Elsa," she said. "It's a family name of long standing." She laughed as if at a joke, but didn't explain any more as she led them to an aged four wheel drive. There was a very happy large German Shepherd dog in the passenger seat. "And this is Danny. Another family name. Shift over, Danny."

Wiggo got in the passenger seat and the other two got in back. Danny, meanwhile, made sure he was firmly lodged between Wiggo and the woman. The dog looked friendly enough, but Wiggo was smart enough to know loyalty when he saw it and made sure to make no sudden moves as Elsa started up the vehicle.

"We're going about ten miles up a valley," she said.

Wiggo eyed the weather cautiously. It was still snowing, and the road was already white. Elsa saw him looking and laughed.

"This is nothing. We'll be fine. And with luck we'll be back at the bar getting some more beer into us long before closing time."

"I'll drink to that," Wiggo said.

She handled the vehicle like a pro, and she was right, the snow was mostly thin and no trouble for them to get through, although the old windscreen wipers weren't coping all that well with the fall. She spoke as she drove, filling in a bit more of the history, but it all seemed rather far fetched to Wiggo. Beasties he could deal with, but talk of relict civilizations...people even...down in the depths of the caves seemed just too much to swallow. Then he remembered Patagonia, and started to revise his thinking accordingly.

"So, Templar treasure? Like in the films?" Wilkins said from the back seat.

"Well, maybe not National Treasure levels of stuff," Elsa replied with a light laugh. "But Great-Great-Grandad always insisted there was a huge pile of gold and jewels."

"Guarded by a dragon, right?"

She laughed again.

"Yes. That's what the old man said, even into his dotage. You can see how the ideas turned a young girl's head, even back then, and even getting them second hand from the old man's grandson, my grandfather. But it's not the treasure I'm interested in. It's the ecosystem. If it's there, it needs to be studied. But more than that, it needs to be protected."

"But first you have to prove it exists?"

"Exactly."

"And where do we come in?" Wiggo said.

"Right about now," she answered, and drove the vehicle off the road and two hundred yards up a rutted track, bringing it to a halt in a clearing only just big enough to hold the vehicle.

She left the lights on and they all went out to see what they were shining on. To Wiggo's eye it looked like no more than a hole in the ground, with a crude set of muddy steps leading down into deep darkness.

"It's a hole," he said. "I've seen one afore."

Elsa laughed again.

"Not like this you haven't. This is where Great-Great-Granddad and his companions came back up out of the earth. 'Resurrected on the third day' he always said. This was their way out. It's our way in."

"Wait a minute, lass. You never said anything about mounting an expedition. We're not equipped."

"I only want to go a small way down, a few steps, that's all, and take some pictures," she said. She went to the rear of the vehicle and returned with a small backpack and a camera slung around her neck. "There's a wider cave just ten feet down with carvings on the walls. I was down just last week but without the camera. I want to go down again."

"Don't let us stop you, lass. Have at it," Wiggo said.

She gave him the big soft eyes again.

"I thought you might want a look for yourself. To satisfy your professional curiosity, after getting the brush-off from Kaminski."

"Oh, professional curiosity is it, now? And here I was thinking you were just feert to go in on your own."

He held up a hand to stop her protests.

"Dinna fret, lass. We've come this far. We'll go and have a keek with you. Yon sad auld bear didnae kill all that livestock. I know it, you know it, and I'm betting Kaminski knows it. If there's something else prowling about, best for everyone if we nip it in the bud early."

He wasn't sure the Cap back in Lossiemouth would agree with his decision, but they'd told him he was on his own.

So I'll do it my way, if it's to be done at all.

He looked down at the hole. It was pitch black below his feet.

"But I didnae bring my torch. I'm not about to go down in the dark, even with a bonnie lass by my side."

She smiled and dug into her backpack, coming up with four headbands with attached lights.

"I thought these might come in handy. They're recharged. Good for a couple of hours at least."

"You've covered everything, haven't you?"

"I hope so," she said solemnly. "I've thought of little else these past few days."

She moved to step down into the hole. The dog took his place by her side, ready to follow, but Wiggo held her back.

"I'll go first," he said. "I like to have something extra along for possible first encounters."

He passed out the head-lights, put his on, unholstered his weapon, held it in his right hand, and, using his left to steady himself, went down into the dark.

Elsa and the dog came right behind him, with the two lads bringing up the rear. It was a tight, narrow space, hardly wider than his shoulders, and it went down steeply, with only more darkness to be seen beneath him when he looked down. He took it carefully, mindful of the damp muddy steps underfoot and the obvious danger of sliding on his arse down into some unknown depths.

He'd gone maybe a dozen steps down when he felt fresher air coming up from below and his hunch they were getting somewhere was confirmed when he spoke and heard a definite resonant echo in his voice as if there was open space close by.

"How far did you say it was, lass?"

"Half a dozen more steps for you," came the reply, and that too was confirmed when he stepped down onto more solid ground and his light showed him to be in a chamber of some kind, obviously man-made given the worked stone and the etchings on the wall.

He stepped aside to let the others descend and soon all four, and the dog, stood looking around the room.

Wilkins whistled softly.

"This is old. Very old."

"I don't think we know the half of it," Elsa replied. She began taking pictures of the pictographs on the walls. The flashing was annoying Wiggo so he turned his back on it and stepped towards the far wall. He felt a breeze, warm, on his face and stepped closer. It was only then he saw that what he'd taken for an alcove was actually a passageway and another narrow set of steps, stone this time, going down into the darkness.

"Where does this go?" he said to Elsa.

"Down," she replied, and laughed again. "They go down. The old man said they climbed up a long way during their escape. I don't think we should be messing with that. Not tonight anyway."

"Now there's something we at least agree on," Wiggo said. "You got your photies?"

Elsa nodded. At the same moment the dog, Danny, moved quickly to the alcove where Wiggo stood and sniffed at the air. The hackles at the back of its neck rose and its lips curled back in a snarl as a deep growl rose in its chest.

"What is it, boy?" Elsa said.

"Trouble is what it is," Wiggo replied. "Marines, we are leaving. Wilko, take point. Back up top and be sharp about it. We'll be right behind you."

That was the plan, but it was scuppered straight away when Danny barked, once, then launched himself off and away down the alcove steps. Elsa almost threw Wiggo aside in her rush to follow him and she too could be heard, footsteps on stone and pained yells of the dog's name echoing back up from below.

"Fucking marvelous," Wiggo muttered, then turned to the other two. "Well, don't just stand there like glaikit hens. Get after her."

He didn't wait for them. He headed at full speed into the alcove.

-3-

The only good thing about the situation was that the stone steps going down were dry underfoot, but Elsa's shouting was receding quicker into the deep than Wiggo and the others could keep up with and soon there was only silence below.

He refrained from calling out, concentrating on his feet and on not missing a step. He heard the other two scuffling down behind him. His head-light illuminated more worked stone, dry and clear of any sign of damp, although the further he descended the more he was sure he could now smell smoke in the air, and a burnt taste at the back of his throat.

After five minutes he came to another chamber, this one circular and larger, being some twelve feet in diameter. There was a window to his right, and he was amazed to see that thin light showed in its frame. He stopped, intending to listen for signs that Elsa might be near. At the same time he stepped towards the window. He looked out over what looked to be a densely forested area in a huge cave under a high roof that appeared to be lit from within in some manner he couldn't fathom. The forest, which appeared to be composed of something very like giant rhubarb, stretched away into dim distance, and the only other thing of note was a squat, obviously man-made pyramid of black stone some miles distant. There was no sign of life; no birds flew, nothing moved among the greenery, not even a breeze, and it felt more like looking at a painting than at a living view.

He only managed to drag his gaze away when Wilkins and Mac arrived beside him.

"Any sign of her?" Wilkins asked, and was answered by insistent barking from somewhere far below. The barking continued as Wiggo once again made for the stairwell heading down.

The stairwell was wider here, and there was definitely dim light below, enough that he could see several steps ahead of him and allow him to move faster, almost at a run. The barking was getting louder, nearer, but now there was a frenzied tone to it, as if the dog was in trouble.

"Hold on," Wiggo muttered. "Just hold on. We're coming."

The light grew brighter still and a minute later he emerged into a much larger room. A balcony looked out over a wider view but he had no time for that; Elsa was backed tight into a corner and only Danny's barking was holding at bay two pale things with long bodies and horse-like heads that were trying to get past the frenzied defense the dog was putting up.

Wiggo's aim and fire came by instinct, the sound of the shot echoing like cannon fire in the room as the nearer of the two beasts fell, its head turned to a bloody mush of greenish pulp. The second turned its attention to him, but by then Wilko and Mac had arrived at his back. Both fired almost simultaneously and the second beast went the way of the first, its head almost completely obliterated. Danny barked excitedly, twice, then raised a leg and pissed over the nearest of the two bodies.

"Good dog," Wiggo said, and looked past it to where Elsa still cowered in the corner. "Any more of those buggers about?" he said as he stepped over and put out a hand. She took it and let him drag her upright before shaking her head.

"Danny flushed them out, but they came after me before I could run. Then all I could do was keep behind him and wait for you; I knew you wouldn't be far behind me."

She already had her composure back and had raised the camera, the flash almost blinding Wiggo as she took a series of photos of the slain beasts from every conceivable angle. While she was busy Wiggo had a long look at them. They were exactly as had been mentioned in the police report; almost barrel-like bodies, long necks, longer tails which made them almost seven feet long from end to end, three legs on each side and heads that were almost horse-like except for the rows of pointed teeth in the jaws. There were also three sharp talons on each foot; these beasts were built for rending flesh and he could now easily imagine what manner of thing had got in among the cattle in the pen.

"What the fuck are they?" Mac asked, kicking at one with his boot.

"Something old," Elsa replied. "You see their like in heraldic crests from the Middle Ages. Wyrms, serpents…dragons? Take your pick, but I think some of them have been coming out of these caverns for a very long time indeed."

"Are ye done, lass?" Wiggo said. "This was supposed to be a short stay, remember? And there's a beer with my name on it back at the Inn."

She wasn't paying attention. She stared over his left shoulder, and Wiggo realized she was seeing the view over the balcony for the first time. He hadn't had a look for himself yet, but whatever she saw, it had made her eyes go wide with wonder. He turned to take a look for himself.

They were in a high spot built into a side of a colossal cave, looking out over a vast plain.

It had once been a city, that was plain from the obviously planned layout of streets and buildings. At some point it had been ravaged, whether by time or fire it was hard to tell, but given the blackening of stone and the winding river of what looked like cooled lava that ran through the center of the area, Wiggo's guess was that the fire was more recent. And now that he'd noticed it he saw the signs everywhere, in smoke-charred walls and a definite burnt smell in the air. Again there was no sign of life; nothing moved but them, high up in their garret viewpoint.

"This place has been dead for decades," Wilkins said at Wiggo's side.

"About a hundred years," Elsa replied, once again busy with the camera, "if the old man's tales are to be believed."

"In that case," Wiggo replied, turning his attention back to the dead beasts, "where did these buggers come from?"

"There are other caverns," Elsa said. "A whole network, maybe even a whole underworld of them. As I said before, it's a lost, or forgotten, ecosystem."

"Aye? Well, maybe for the best if it stays lost," Wiggo answered, and gave the nearest body a kick. "Now, are we going or what?"

Once again Danny had other ideas. The dog moved to the foot of the stairwell, raised his nose, sniffed, then let out a long, wailing howl as the hackles once again rose at his neck.

"What fuckery is this now?" Wiggo said.

They all heard it coming, the clitter-clatter of talons scratching on stone and a high hissing sound, like a group of angry cats. It was coming from somewhere above them, in the stairwell. Wilkins was closest to the stairs. He poked his head in and looked up, then quickly withdrew, at the same time unholstering his pistol.

"How many?" Wiggo asked.

"All of them, I think," Wilkins replied. "We're not getting out that way in a hurry."

Wiggo turned to Mac.

"See if you can find us a safe exit point," he said. "Or at least somewhere we can hold defensively for a while."

"What about me?" Elsa said.

"Stay behind me. And keep Danny quiet. I don't want him getting in our line of fire."

He went to join Wilkins at the foot of the stairs. The clicking of talons on stone was close now, and the hissing sounded somehow eager and excited.

"Let's see what they're made of," Wiggo said, and raised his pistol. "On three."

He counted down, stepped forward into the stairwell and looked up. They were directly above him, half a dozen or more crawling, heads downward, filling up all the space, hissing vehemently when they caught sight of him. Wilko stepped up at his side and they both fired, round after round. A body fell down the steps towards them, forcing Wiggo, then Wilkins to retreat a step. The scurry of talons on rock got louder and the hissing turned to shrieking wails. Behind them Danny started to howl in accompaniment. Wiggo could only hope that Elsa could control him as he and Wilkins pumped more shots up the stairwell.

Two more bodies fell at their feet, but the sheer weight and bulk of them meant that they had to take yet another step back, precluding them from being able to fire up the stairwell. More beasts kept coming from above, the noise level rising as the attackers sensed the nearness of fresh prey.

"This isn't working," Wiggo said. He turned, looking for Mac. "Anything?" he called out.

"Maybe. But it's risky," Mac called back.

The screeching noise from the stairwell reached a cacophony. Elsa had Danny by the neck but was clearly struggling to hold him back; it was only a matter of time before the dog launched itself into the fray, and there would only be one outcome from that. A messy one.

"So is this, lad. Where do we go?"

"Follow me."

Wiggo motioned to Elsa that she should comply, and was pleased to get an immediate nod in return. She followed Mac off to their right where there was a doorway out of the chamber.

Wilkins still stood at the foot of the stairwell. Two beasts showed their heads in the doorway. He took them both out, single shots between the eyes. Their bodies fell to join the growing pile on the floor even as the noise continued to intensify above them.

"Can't hold them much longer, Sarge," Wilkins said.

"Back off, to me, slowly," Wiggo said. "I've got you covered."

Wilkins backed off. Wiggo took out another beast that dared to show itself and started backing off himself. Mac shouted from the door at the left.

"To me. I'll cover you."

They backed away quickly. The stairwell rapidly filled with wailing, squirming beasts. One of them dashed out into the chamber. Mac took it down, but it took two shots and that gave more of them time to emerge.

"This way," Mac shouted. Wiggo let Wilkins go ahead of him and watched the rear as the others went through the doorway. He emptied his clip into the squirming mass of beasts that were leaking into the chamber from the stairwell, then turned and followed, reloading as he went.

Mac led them out into the open air, and onto a wooden walkway that led in a ten meter bridge across a deep chasm to what looked to be a forest of giant rhubarb on the far side. Wiggo guessed it might even be the same one he'd seen from the window higher up, but he had no time to think about it. Mac, Elsa and the dog were already on the opposite side, and

Mac was busy kicking at the timbers where the walkway was fitted into the clifftop, obviously intent on sending the whole thing tumbling into the chasm. Wilkins had almost made it all the way across. He turned and shouted at Wiggo.

"Move your arse, Sarge. They're coming."

Wiggo wasn't about to make the mistake of looking back. He pumped his legs and ran full pelt across the walkway, and was almost at the far side when he saw Wilkins kneel and take aim.

"Get down, Sarge," the corporal shouted, and Wiggo threw himself face down on the wood. Two shots zinged overhead, then he felt a strong arm grab him by the wrist and drag him to his feet. Mac and the woman were gouging and digging at the fastenings of the bridge, and had one side loose. Wiggo looked back. Three of the beasts were coming forward fast onto the walkway, with more gathering at their back. He weighed the options, decided escape was the better plan, and went to help Mac, leaving Wilkins to watch the bridge.

It took a lot of tugging and kicking, and there were four dead beasts on the bridge with six more crawling on top of the bodies when the near end of the walkway's foundations finally gave way beneath their feet and the whole bridge swung away, falling into the chasm and taking the screaming beasts down with them. A dozen beasts remained on the cliff on the far side, but they appeared to lose interest and in a matter of minutes they too had dispersed.

Wiggo looked across the chasm to the doorway into the chambers beyond, then up, and up, an impossibly high cliff face to a ceiling high overhead. Below his feet was nothing but chasm, and at his back nothing but the fleshy giant-leaved forest. There was no way he could see for them to get back up to where they had come in.

"Well, isn't this just fucking marvelous?" he said.

-4-

Captain John Banks was trying to control his anger, but if it had been possible to punch someone through a laptop screen he'd have been more than willing to give it a try.

"What do you mean, missing?" he said.

He'd been woken in the early hours of the morning to take an urgent call so wasn't in the best of moods in any case, and this smug German, Kaminski, wasn't making it any better.

"They are not in their rooms in the inn," the German policeman said. "And they were last seen in the company of Elsa Brunke, a known local troublemaker and conspiracy theorist. We found her vehicle in the woods near what is known to be an entrance to a cave system, but there is no sign of either her or your men in the area. I can only assume that, against my instructions, they went down into the system with her."

"Then get somebody down there after them," Banks said, stifling a shout.

"I cannot do that," Kaminski said. "We have no one with the training necessary and besides…"

"Besides, you don't really give a fuck about three British soldiers and a local nutjob? Is that it?"

Kaminski smiled thinly but didn't reply.

"I'm coming over," Banks said.

"You will have no jurisdiction," Kaminski replied.

"Fuck the red tape. My men might be in trouble."

"You will, of course, do what you have to do," Kaminski said. "But I cannot offer any assistance. You must understand… my hands are tied."

"Pity it wasn't your mouth," Banks said, and switched off the call before he could make things even worse.

"You fucked up, Wiggo, didn't you, lad?" he muttered, then went to get dressed, He had some phone calls to make, and much to do.

One advantage of his current position was that he could give orders without having to explain them or have anyone questioning them. Three hours later he was at the base, getting ready to board a plane to Salzburg, waiting only for the arrival of his chosen wing-man for the op.

He'd considered taking a full team, but swinging that at this hour was going to draw attention he didn't need. His hope was to get over to the cave system, fetch the squad out and be home before anyone of note took notice. To make that work he had to go quick and quiet, so decided on just one man, a lad he knew to be reliable.

Lieutenant Joe Duffield was a bit of a rising star in Lossiemouth and Banks knew the colonel thought very highly of him. He'd also got form in the right areas, having been on the clean-up squad after the mess in London and been team leader mopping up in the Yukatan. The lad already knew monsters existed, so there wasn't going to be the whole 'is it really true?' conversation that got wearing after the tenth time, and he was as keen as mustard, despite getting dragged from bed at an ungodly hour, when Banks asked him to be his wing-man on the mission.

He was coming down from digs in Inverness by taxi, and Banks was just starting to wonder if it had been delayed when it arrived at the gates of the base and was passed through. A couple of minutes later Duffield joined him in the hold of the cargo plane.

"So what is it, Cap?" the young officer asked. He was a sturdily built chap, played rugby in his spare time, was built like a bull across the shoulders, but fresh-faced with it, showing a wide grin and an oft-used smile. He was twenty-four years old but the grin made him look a couple of years younger, and Banks was already having second thoughts about taking him along into what was, after all, a descent into the unknown. But it was all he was going to be able to muster at such short notice, and time was wasting.

He ordered the pilot to take off, then motioned Duffield to a seat. As Banks sat down he kicked at two hefty kit-bags at his feet.

"This is all the gear I could wangle at such short notice. I hope it's enough. Done any caving or pot-holing, lad?" he asked, then filled Duffield in on the situation at hand.

"Do you think they're onto something, Wiggo and the others?" Duffield asked when Banks was done.

"Well, Wiggo's onto a kick up his arse when I see him," Banks replied. "But as for anything else, we just don't know. We're going in blind on this one, and with no backup."

"Par for the course for you and the lads, isn't it?"

"I suppose so. But I'm usually there when we all do something fucking stupid. It's not the same looking on from the outside."

"Do you think they're in trouble?"

"It's Wiggo. Of course they're in trouble. He's a shite-magnet."

Then there was nothing more he could do but worry as the plane headed east into the approaching dawn.

-5-

They'd been walking through the giant-leaved forest for a while and getting nowhere fast when Wiggo called them to a halt in a small clearing.

"Bugger this for a lark," he said. "We need to get back up top, and we need to do it fast. Anybody got any bright ideas?"

"I have one," Elsa replied, "but I'm not sure you're going to like it."

"Let's hear it, lass. Anything's going to be better than more of this green shite."

"We let Danny lead us. He knows the quickest way home from anywhere within twenty miles. His nose will find us a way out."

Danny barked softly as if in confirmation, and Wiggo could only laugh.

"It's as good an idea as any I've got," he said. He looked to Wilkins and Mac. "You got anything better?"

"Short of trying to get back across yon chasm..." Wilkins started.

"...and back into the middle of a pack of whatever the fuck those things are? I think not," Wiggo replied. "At least the beasties don't seem to be over here. That's the only plus point of this trip so far."

The forest had proved to be a bland monoculture from what they'd seen of it, with no life apart from an endless field of the giant fleshy stems topped with umbrella-sized leaves that hung in a damp canopy a couple of feet overhead and lent everything a greenish tinge, even in the dim light.

At least there was light. Elsa surmised it was some kind of bioluminescence in vegetation growing on the ceiling. All Wiggo knew was that it gave them an artificial daylight that showed no signs of dimming. Elsa had also dug in her rucksack and come out with a bottle of filtered water and a large bar of chocolate, which, as of that moment, was their only source of sustenance. Wiggo was going to have to do something about that situation soon if a way out wasn't forthcoming.

He looked down at the dog, which looked back at him and wagged its tail, as if eager to please.

"Fuck it. We'll go with the dog," he said, and turned to Elsa. "Do your thing."

Elsa bent down and took the dog's head between her hands.

"Home, Danny. Take us home," she said.

Danny barked once, enthusiastically, then headed off towards Wiggo's left. He stopped on the edge of the canopy, looked back, then barked again.

"There you go, lads," Wiggo said. "Follow the leader."

As one they followed the dog into the forest.

Danny seemed keen to forge ahead, and kept stopping to bark frustratedly at them for their lack of speed, but it was slow going amid the giant stems for there was no defined pathway and they often had to squeeze through tightly packed foliage to follow the dog's trail.

Wiggo lit up a smoke, his first since their descent. He'd been loath to do anything that might attract the attention of more of the six-legged beasts, but they had seen nothing to suggest that this was any more than a single expanse of forest, with no animal spoor or tracks to indicate that anything else frequented the area. While he walked he was mulling over his decisions that had led them to this juncture, but honestly couldn't see how he would have done anything differently at any point along the line; the woman needed help, he helped. It was part of what made him the man he was, and if the Cap or the brass saw that as a failing on his part, well, fuck 'em, he wasn't about to change his character for a pat-on-the-back promotion that would mean little but a wee bit extra in the bank every month. What he was worried about was that he had led Wilkins and Mac along with him, and not had a single complaint. He owed it to them to now get them out of here in one piece, although he still wasn't sure that relying on a dog to do that for him was the best plan of action.

He was still lost in thought when Danny barked excitedly somewhere ahead of him. Wiggo pushed his way through the fronds and was amazed to come out into open air. Danny stood in the middle of what gave every impression of being an old paved walkway, his tail wagging and an expression on his face that told everyone how pleased he was of himself.

"Good lad," Wiggo said, and Danny came over for a chuck under the chin before returning to Elsa's side.

Wiggo looked both ways along the paved path. It was ten paces wide, and seemed to cut a straight swathe right through the heart of the greenery. The stones that made up the path were regularly cut, about the same shape and design as those of the cobbled streets of old Edinburgh and completely free of any moss or weed. The join between each was so tight Wiggo thought he wouldn't even get a cigarette paper in between them. The path stretched as far as he could see in either direction, fading into a misty gloom in the distance. If they were in the same cave he had seen from the high window there would be a black pyramid here somewhere, but as yet it could not be seen.

"Which way now, Danny?" he said.

The dog had, for the moment at least, lost interest, and was intent on bothering Elsa, trying to root around in her backpack after a treat. But at least he'd brought them out of the forest. Wiggo's gloomy mood had lifted, if only a bit, with the feel of fresher air in his face and the more open aspect without the looming canopy immediately overhead.

"Follow the Yellow Brick Road," he said. "I wonder if there's a wee man behind a curtain at the end of the line?" He pointed left. "May as well keep going in the same general direction as Danny's first thought. And keep your eyes peeled for either fresh water or something to eat; we're going to need both soon."

Elsa came to his side as they headed out again.

"I have to say, you're all taking all of this rather calmly," she said.

"I could say the same of you, lass," Wiggo replied. "We've got form when it comes to dealing with really weird shite. What's your excuse?"

She smiled.

"It doesn't seem strange to me because I've been hearing the stories all of my life, passed down from the old man who was here all those years ago. It's actually gratifying to finally know they were not just stories."

"Is there anything at all in yon stories about how we might get out of here?"

"I've been thinking about that. Nothing of help, I'm afraid. They got out the way we came in. And the way they got in, through that big cave above the cattle pens, was blocked off by flood and fire even while they were here."

"And yet the beasties were at that cattle pen… which suggests they came out of that cave, does it not?"

She shrugged.

"I can't explain it. But it's not as if there's a map to follow. There's no way for us to know how to get there from here anyway. I don't even know if we're heading back towards where we left the truck, or away from it."

"My gut tells me we're heading in the right general direction," Wiggo said, "and I can usually trust it. And if you don't trust me, trust Danny… we're going the way he wanted to go."

"Yes. But he's probably just following the smell of food," she said, laughing.

"And there's nothing wrong with that," Wiggo replied.

Elsa was about to add something, but Wiggo put a finger to his lips. Danny had stopped in the middle of the path and had his nose in the air, looking upwards. Wiggo followed the dog's gaze. There was a darker patch up in the roof, one that appeared to be shifting, as if alive.

Elsa looked up, then pulled at his arm.

"We need to get back under cover," she said, and for the first time since she was cornered in the chamber he saw fear in her eyes. "The old man spoke of this."

"Not good?"

"Not in the slightest."

"You heard the lady," Wiggo said. "Get off the road, lads. There's trouble in the air."

In the air was right, for just at that point Danny barked loudly and the dark spot in the ceiling broke apart into a score and more different darker spots. It was only when they opened their wings that Wiggo noticed they were some kind of very large bat. And just as he had noticed them, they had noticed the people on the road.

The bats all turned as one into a diving attack, coming straight for the road.

They scattered; Wiggo ended up on one side of the path with Elsa and Danny, with Wilkins and Mac on the far side from them. Elsa was frantically tugging at Wiggo's jacket, trying to get him to move further back under the foliage, but Wiggo stood for several seconds, intent on getting a close look at this new attack.

He saw immediately that the distance had led him to underestimate the sheer size of the approaching beasts; they looked to have a wingspan of at least nine feet, and their bodies were almost man-sized, if not man-shaped. They had four limbs apart from the wings, and all seemed to be equipped with sharp talons. Their heads were more dog-like than horse-like, but like the wyrms earlier, these too had long, whipping tails which looked to be acting like foils and flaps to aid in the things' flight. They swooped in formation like a squad of dive-bombers, and when the lead one began to shriek the others joined in, filling the air with a cacophonous wail.

He'd also underestimated both the distance between him and the attack, and the speed with which it approached. Elsa yelled out and threw herself flat on the ground with Danny beneath her. Wiggo was almost too late in joining her, and later was sure that he'd felt a talon touch his woolen hat as he'd tumbled aside, rolling onto his back as he moved and bringing up his pistol.

The bat screamed in frustration at missing its target.

Wiggo screamed back at it, and took careful aim.

"One up the jacksie is as good as one in the head," he muttered, and put a bullet into the back end of the bat-thing even as it passed him. He had to roll again immediately as two more of the bats swooped immediately above him, talons reaching but failing to find him. He didn't see the result of his shot; but he heard it; a crash of something soft hitting cobblestone, and the crack of bones breaking.

Wiggo rolled away to end up beside Elsa and the dog under the canopy then looked back out onto the causeway.

The attacking bats had forgotten all about the men; a frenzied mob descended like locusts onto the broken body of their erstwhile leader and were rending it into ever smaller parts even as its death squeals pierced the air with its agony.

Wiggo saw Mac raise his pistol, taking aim at one of the feeding bats. He caught Mac's eye and motioned for him to put the gun down; if it was a toss up between drawing more attention to themselves or staying hidden, Wiggo chose, this time, to keep a low profile.

They cowered under the canopy in silence and watched the bats at their messy feast.

-6-

Banks, with Duffield at his side, stood looking down into a hole in the ground, one that was almost totally covered in a new fall of snow. A 4x4, the woman's if the local cops were right, was parked off to one side. Kaminski had been fair-minded enough to send a car to the airport for them, but that was as far as his hospitality was going to stretch, and their taciturn driver had departed five minutes ago, leaving them alone in a cold, fresh morning.

"I've been down a few holes in the Yorkshire Moors," Duffield said. "But nothing serious. How about you, Cap?"

"About the same," Banks replied. "But a lot longer ago than you. Still, there's no use losing time worrying about it. Let's get kitted up and get down there. The lads might need us."

He'd brought only what he thought were necessities in the kits bags; each of them had a rifle and spare ammo on a belt, a handgun on a hip holster and a large knife in a scabbard. Apart from that, they each wore a jacket fitted with a light harness and they had a hundred feet of climbing rope in a tight coil tied at their backs, alongside a small pouch of carabiners and pegs and a climbing hammer. There was one small bag containing a basic medical kit, which Duffield stowed with the rope at his back. The outfit was topped off with a hard helmet mounted with a strong flashlight. He'd brought spare batteries for them which Banks stowed in his belt but hoped they would never be needed. He also had a canteen of water, which he attached to his belt.

After donning all the gear he looked down again at the hole below them.

It was going to be a tight squeeze, and hard work. Besides that, his leg was already starting to squeal its pain at him. He pushed that down as far as he could manage at the back of his mind.

"Ready?" he said to Duffield.

"As I'll ever be, Cap," the lad replied. Banks clapped him on the shoulder then lowered himself into the hole.

It was every bit as tight as he'd imagined, and at several points he had to twist and turn before he could slip downwards. There were rough steps underfoot, but they were wet. Thick mud slipped and slid underfoot even despite the benefit of the treads of his heavy boots and he was all too aware that at any moment he might lose grip and fall away down into darkness. He was relieved when he felt fresher air coming up from below and descended down a minute later into a drier chamber, but less relieved to note that this place, despite being at least ten meters underground, was obviously man-made and of ancient construction. It was also empty, but there were muddy footprints on the floor, a great many of them, along with what looked like paw prints made by a large dog.

Duffield came down to join him. With both their lights on the chamber was well enough lit for them to see all around it. The fresher air was coming from an alcove off to the right. Banks stepped over and felt a breeze on his face, and saw that it came up from another set of steps, fashioned of worked stone of similar age to the walls of the chamber. There was no sound coming up from the depths.

He pointed down, and motioned for Duffield to follow. From now on they were going to silent running; who knew what might be waiting for them, down in the dark?

The descent was easier on this second stretch, the stone firm and dry underfoot. The fresher air didn't last however. The further he descended the more Banks was sure he smelled something else in the air, an acrid tang that reminded him of nothing less than death and corruption. The smell was even more evident when they stepped out of the stairwell and into a larger chamber. The steps continued downward through an exit on the far side, but Banks was more interested in the fact that there was now a source of light other than his headlamp, and it came from a tall window. He stepped over and looked out over a huge cavern, the floor of which was covered in a dense carpet of vegetation. Some bird-like things flew in the distance, mere black specks, spiraling above a great black pyramid, but still there was no sound, and only the faintest of breezes coming in from the outside. If his squad was down there, they were lost from sight somewhere in the vegetation. Banks took no sense of wonder from the view, only a deep and growing frustration.

"What the fuck have you got yourself into this time, Wiggo?" he muttered.

When he moved away from the window the tang of corruption was once again obvious. It was definitely coming up the stairwell from somewhere below. When he moved in that direction he was pleased to note that Duffield followed close at his back without being prompted. The lad's grin had gone now, and with his game-face on he looked more like a soldier than a boy, which Banks could only take as a good sign; he had a feeling he was going to be needing that soldier sooner rather than later.

The smell got steadily worse the further down they descended. The reason became apparent when they reached another chamber and found their exit from the stairwell blocked by the bodies of half a dozen dead beasts. Banks recognized them from the description that had been in the briefing papers he gave Wiggo, but that bald text hadn't done justice to the obvious ferocity of the beasts, even in death. Nor had it given any indication of the stench. He had to cover his mouth with one hand while kicking the corpses aside, trying in vain to keep the wash of blood and body fluids from getting on his boots and trousers.

He was about to push through into the chamber beyond when he realized, almost too late, that the beast immediately underfoot wasn't dead; it had its head buried in the belly of one of its kin, and it was feeding. It raised its head, gore dripping from a bloody snout, and two pale, almost silver, eyes blinked and focused on Banks.

He was already falling backwards when it lunged for him, jaws snapping only an inch from his heels. It came forward using its rear legs and tail like a piston, a snake-like strike, heading for his groin. Banks wasn't going to have time to aim and fire, so resorted to using the weapon as a club, but it was like striking a lump of cold stone, and had about as little effect. The thing's jaws opened, ready to clamp down.

A shot roared out, like a cannon going off near his ear, and the thing's head fell in on itself like a burst football. The heavy body fell full onto Banks' legs, bringing a fresh flare of pain in the old wound. Duffield stepped up and kicked the new corpse aside before helping Banks to his feet. There was no time for him to thank the lad. Loud scurrying and the scratch of talons on stone told of activity in the chamber beyond. Something hissed loudly, and was replied to by several others, a noise that quickly rose to an insistent screaming that echoed up the stairwell.

Banks chanced a look. The floor of the chamber beyond was strewn with dead beasts, and others of their kind very much still alive, a dozen or more, who had obviously been feeding. Unfortunately their attention was now laser-focused on the doorway where the two men stood. The only good thing about the view was that there was no sign of the squad or the woman, and that the dead beasts showed clear signs of being killed by small weapons fire. The lads had been here, but had moved on. Banks thought it was about time he did the same, but could see no way they could make it across the chamber without getting into a fight in which the odds would be stacked against them.

"Back up the stairs, lad," he said softly. "No sudden moves, but make it sharpish. We've got no chance here if they all come at once."

The beasts watched, unmoving as first Duffield then Banks stepped backwards, one, then two steps up. As if a switch had been thrown or a silent command given, the beasts came forward as one, scuttling towards the doorway, getting in each others' way in a suddenly frantic lunge for the men.

"Faster, lad. Get to the top of the flight. We'll have to try to hold them there."

The two men kept backing off. As they retreated upwards, the doorway below them quickly filled with a crawling mass of the six-legged beasts, all hissing and squealing as they clambered for space from which they might be able to launch an attack.

Banks' every instinct was to pump a volley of rounds into the mass of beasts, but he had no way of knowing how many more that might attract. He was only too aware that retreating was only delaying a decision, but his plan all along had been to move softly and quietly; getting into a gunfight with a gang of vicious beasts hadn't been on his agenda.

But the decision was taken out of his hands in any case. Duffield spoke softly from the step above.

"We've got trouble, Cap. There's something moving in the stairwell up above."

"Human?"

"I don't think so."

They heard it soon afterwards, the tell-tale scratch of talons on stone and a high hiss as if of triumph, soon joined by others, both from above and below.

They were trapped.

-7-

The bat-things seemed to take an age at their feast, giving Wiggo ample opportunity to study them. They were definitely more dog-like than the wyrms they'd seen earlier, with almost canine faces and ears, although their tails told of a more reptilian lineage, being thick and rough-scaled. While on the ground they had their wings tucked tight to their flanks but he saw enough to know that they were thin, almost membranous and shot through with pulsing blue veins, and when they opened out they stretched almost nine feet from tip to tip.

He was still watching the bats when Danny's ears perked up. There was a distant crack, which might have been wood breaking or might have been gunfire, but it only happened once and Wiggo was reluctant to decide either way; it wasn't as if they were in any position to go and investigate.

And still the bats feasted until, finally, as if gorged, they took off, flapping clumsily at first until they got air under them, then soaring as one off and away, high up to their roosting spot in the roof. Even then Wiggo waited until all movement up there stopped and there was only a darker gray patch showing before motioning to the others that they were safe to leave the canopy.

Danny came out from his place under Elsa, wandered over to the remains of the bat, sniffed once, then lifted a leg and pissed on the deflated bag of bones and skin that was all that remained of the thing.

"I'll say one thing for that dog," Wiggo said, "it's got good taste."

Wiggo looked both ways along the cobbled pathway. There was still no sign of life in either direction. A look upwards confirmed that all was quiet overhead.

"We have to stick to this path if we want to make good time, but everybody keep their eyes peeled; those buggers can come down like bullets, so we want to know they're coming. Stay near the path edge where you can, and get under cover at the first sign of trouble. Everybody with me?"

He got OK signals from both Mac and Wilkins and a thumbs up from Elsa. Danny wagged his tail, so Wiggo took that as a full house, and pointed off to his right.

"We go thataway. Double time."

They got their first sight of the pyramid twenty minutes later, a squat black thing directly ahead of them on the path, which looked to have been built for the express purpose of leading the way there. There had been more bats overhead along the way, but they had been circling lazily high up near the roof, and none had shown any dive-bombing inclinations. Wiggo had taken advantage of that by keeping everyone moving along quickly, almost at a trot, but had to slow them down when Elsa started to tire.

"You're forgetting, I'm not a soldier," she said between gasps. "The most exercise I've ever done is trying to catch my morning train."

Her build belied that statement, and Wiggo guessed that, as a country lass, she was generally pretty fit in any case, but she was clearly out of breath so it was a moot point anyway. He called a halt and took the opportunity for a smoke break while keeping one eye on the bats above and the other on the black pyramid. From this distance, somewhere over a mile away, it looked as dead and empty as the chambers in the mountainside they'd been in earlier, but he knew enough now not to take anything for granted. He did have one question though.

"So who the fuck built all this stuff then? And when?"

Elsa shrugged.

"Old Stefan said there were people down here, well, as near to people as made little difference."

"Well, there's none now."

"Not that we've seen," Elsa replied. "But as I said… these cave systems are extensive. There's a lot of room for them to hide in."

"If the fire didn't get them, or the beasties ate the survivors, or…"

Elsa nodded again.

"We might never know. Nobody might ever know unless…"

"Unless I find us a way up and out of here? Aye, I ken, lass. I'm working on it. Maybe we should ask the dog again?"

Danny appeared oblivious to any need for his services. He was currently rooting around at the base of one of the fleshy plants, digging with his front paws. His snout went down, and when it came back up he was chewing on something.

"What have you got there, lad?" Wiggo said.

The dog came over and dropped its 'prize' at Wiggo's feet. It was a fat, maggoty thing, three inches long, pale and somewhat greasy, with six stubby legs, a rudimentary tail and a flat face with a rubbery sucker for a mouth. It felt sticky, slightly slimy to the touch and made Wiggo feel queasy just to look at it, but when he dropped it to the ground Danny immediately picked it up and took to chewing again with some gusto.

"If he says it's edible, it's edible," Elsa said.

"Look, lass," Wiggo replied, "I've seen dogs eat another dog's shite. I'm not about to take culinary tips from one of them."

But time was getting on...the rumblings in his belly were testament to that, and hunger would have to be assuaged at some point.

He looked at the mess of the thing that hung half-in, half-out of the dog's mouth.

Just not quite yet.

As they got closer Wiggo looked up the height of the pyramid. It looked like it was almost touching the roof at its topmost point. But there was something else too, a squirming, darker area in a wide patch, another roost of the bat things, and much larger than the one they'd seen before. The path ahead of them led directly to the foot of the pyramid and to a processional set of steps that went up twenty feet or so to a dark opening into the structure's depths.

"Where do you think that goes?" Mac asked.

"Up, lad. It goes up. And so must we. Come on, look sharpish; my stomach's telling me it's supper time, and I'd like a beer with it."

He kept an eye on the gray patch on the roof above, but the roosting things showed no sign of being interested in them.

"At least one thing's gone right for us," he muttered as he took the lead, walked off the path and onto the first step of the pyramid. As soon as his foot hit stone a humming vibration rose all around them and the hair on the back of his neck rose up. Static electricity cracked like a pistol shot. High overhead the bat things stirred and detached themselves from their roosts.

Wiggo's first instinct was to do as they had done before and retreat under the canopy, but Danny was at Elsa's side, his gaze fixed on the vegetation, lips drawn back from his gums and growling deep in his chest; Wiggo didn't take this as a good sign, and almost immediately saw why the dog was agitated. Something…several things…moved in there, more of the low and long pale beasts with heads like horses. There was no telling how many of them might be lying in wait under the greenery.

The bats above, having circled once, launched into their dive, coming fast.

"Fuck," Wiggo said loudly, then turned to the others. "Leg it. Get inside. It's our only hope."

The bat-things screamed as they came, wings folded and dropping like stones. Wilkins and Mac took the lead and were already kneeling in the doorway, pistols aiming upward, looking for a clear shot. Wilkins shouted.

"Get a move on, Sarge. This is going to be close."

The dog barked and snarled, tried to drag itself out of Elsa's reach and, turning, Wiggo saw why; the low, lizard-like things were coming out from under the forest canopy, and had blocked any escape route back towards the roadway.

We're being herded.

Elsa reached the doorway first and Danny finally allowed himself to be coerced and followed her inside to be lost in the shadows behind Wilkins and Mac. Wiggo was three steps down, but wasn't going to make it; two of the bats plunged towards him, wings unfolding, their screams like a storm wind whistling in his ears. He ducked and rolled sideways, taking aim as he looked up. Talons raked the air in front of his face as he put two shots into the bat which fell like a stone at his feet and rolled down the step where the lizard things fell on it in a frenzy. That was all he had time for. A second bat was on him before he could change his aim, its head hitting him in the belly and driving all the wind from him even as talons tore at his groin, only his thick trousers preventing him from being immediately gelded. He smashed the butt of his pistol against the thing's head and rolled over, hoping to pin it beneath him. A calm voice spoke above him.

"I got this, Sarge," Wilkins said. "Close your eyes."

Wiggo did as he was told, A shot boomed near his left ear and the weight of the beast fell away. A strong hand took him by the shoulder and dragged him upright. Using Wilkins as a crutch they staggered up and into the shelter of the doorway. Below them the lizards were tearing into two dead bats, while above the air was a screaming, swooping mass of frenzied wings. A group, a dozen or more, of the lizards were avoiding the feeding frenzy and coming forward, already at the foot of the stairs and heading upward.

"Fight or flee?" Wilkins said.

Wiggo looked behind him. Steps headed upward into the darkness of the pyramid. It looked dark and empty, but still preferable to the chaos immediately outside.

"Let's see if we can find somewhere quiet where I can check if my bollocks are still attached," he said, and motioned Wilkins to take point. He turned for one last look outside. The bats were now circling away upward once more, still screaming. The lizards crowded at the foot of the steps, a mass of at least forty of them varying in size from six to ten feet long, all staring directly at the doorway, hissing loudly like angry cats.

As Wiggo switched on his head-light and turned into the darkness of the pyramid he couldn't shake the feeling that the beasts now had the squad exactly where they wanted them to be.

-8-

Banks was still pondering their next move when his mind was made up for him. Gunfire cracked, somewhere in the distance, but unmistakable.

The lads are in trouble.

"Bugger this for a lark," he muttered, aimed the rifle downwards and pulled the trigger, sending a volley of rounds into the densely packed beasts.

The result was carnage; gore and ichor splashed, limbs were fractured, heads burst open, and the surviving beasts, sent frenzied by bloodlust, tore into their own wounded and dead in a melee, a fury of tooth and claw.

"Watch our backs, lad," Banks said, "and stay behind me. We're going through."

He stepped downward, aiming more carefully now and taking out any still living beasts with clinical shots to the head. When he reached the bloody remains he had to kick some bodies aside, and step warily through a wash of blood and gore, before he was able to stand in the doorway and look into the chamber beyond. Three of the beasts were still alive, intent on feeding. He took them out swiftly with no fuss, stepped out into the now quiet chamber and walked towards the balcony, hoping to escape the stench of death and shite that hung everywhere. He heard Duffield at his back.

"Anything behind us?"

"No, sir. Looks like they buggered off when you started shooting."

"Smart lads," he muttered. He looked out over the balcony to a ruined city and dried lava beds. There was no movement, and only slightly fresher air, for the distinct smell of old fires hung heavy here. If the squad had been here, they were now somewhere else. He checked for a way out, and quickly found a passageway leading to what felt like even fresher air beyond.

"If we were hoping for any element of surprise, I've just buggered that up royally. But it can't be helped. This way, lad," he said. "And hope that if we heard them, they heard us, and we can meet somewhere in the middle."

The passageway brought them around in a semi circle and out onto a high walkway above a ravine. They could see the remnants of what had recently been a bridge across to a green forested area on the other side, but the structure had obviously gone down into the depths, and it was at least fifteen feet across; Banks knew he couldn't make the jump, not with his bad leg. He turned to Duffield to see the lad was already uncoiling his rope.

"Watch my back, Cap. I've got this," he said. He attached the rope to what had been a bridge support, deftly arranged the workings at his harness and less than a minute later was abseiling down into the ravine, obviously a practiced hand at the task. Seconds later he was on the bottom and waving Banks on…

"I've got you covered, Cap," his voice came, echoing slightly along the ravine. Banks checked back along the path; there was no sign of any of the lizards, and no other sound of gunfire in the air. He arranged his harness, carefully lowered himself down to where the rope hung, and hooked himself up before stepping out above the drop.

His gammy leg hurt with every bounce off the face on the way down, but at least it didn't last long, and seconds later he was on the floor of the ravine beside young Duffield.

"Okay, you got us here, lad," he said. "Now what?"

"I've got that covered too, Cap," he said. He asked for Banks' rope, put it over his neck and under one arm, then without another word turned to the face of the cliff below the forested area. He took to climbing. Banks had always thought of himself as a more than reasonable climber, but Duffield was obviously a level or two above; he went up the cliff face as if he didn't even have to look for handholds, just found them instinctively where he put his fingers, all fluid movement and momentum.

Banks heard him scrambling, but knew better than to fix his gaze on the man; he kept his eye on the deep shadows in the floor of the ravine, alert to the slightest movement, but there was no sign of anything alive but himself. He stood on hardened lava, obviously laid down some time ago, for pallid lichens were making their home in cracks in the surface, and there was no residual heat he could feel. But the burnt smell was stronger here; there had been some sort of fiery cataclysm down here in the past, but whatever had happened, anyone who'd been around to see it was long since dead and gone. He put any conjecture on the subject to the back of his mind; the squad was what mattered here, and he wasn't going to be able to rest until they were safe.

All of them.

He jumped when something slapped, hard, against the rock at his back, then heard an echoing voice shout 'Sorry' from above. He turned to see the rope dangling, its end just a foot above the ravine floor. He looked up to see Duffield silhouetted against the paler roof high above. Banks' bad leg flared in pain just at the thought of the next few minutes, but there was no alternative. He gritted his teeth, hooked the rope into his harness in case of a fall, and began to haul himself upward.

Around halfway up he was wishing he'd stayed below. He'd thought the pain in his leg had been bad before, but it was nothing compared to the lancing flare of simultaneous cold and heat that ran from hip to ankle every time he had to use it. He was relying mostly on his arm strength and was making progress; he just wasn't sure he was going to have enough left in the tank to make it all the way. He paused for a breather and looked up; Duffield was there above him, following his progress.

"Heads up, Cap," the younger man shouted. "We've got company on the far side."

Banks turned and looked up at the cliff face on the other side of the ravine. Half a dozen of the long lizards stood where the bridge had been anchored. They were all looking down at him.

I hope to fuck they're not good jumpers.

Turned out, it wasn't their jumping he should have been worrying about. As one, heads downward, they all came down off the edge and started to climb, slowly, sinuously but with no apparent effort, down the side of the cliff. In a matter of a minute or so they'd be below him on the valley floor, and then it was going to be a race to the top.

He didn't like his chances.

"Shall I take them, Cap?" Duffield called.

"Not yet," Banks shouted back, and tried to put on a burst of speed.

He refused to look back, or down, just put all his concentration and effort into the climb. He felt something give in his leg, and got a fresh burst of almost blinding pain for his sins.

"Cap?" Duffield said, from thankfully not too far above; definitely close enough for Banks to hear the anxiety in his voice. "Best hurry."

Banks made the mistake of looking down. Six beasts looked up at him from mere yards below his feet, coming up fast. There was no way he'd get to the top before they were on him.

"Take them," he shouted, and at the same time allowed himself to swing free of the rock face, trusting the harness to hold him as he got the rifle swung round into position from his back. He was almost too slow. Shots rang out from above and two of the beasts, one on each side, fell away squealing, but Banks realized that his body would be directly in Duffield's line of sight, blocking him from the other four.

Here goes nothing.

He aimed as well as he was able, and sprayed off a volley. The recoil sent him back, hard, against the rock, but he took grim pleasure in seeing three of the four remaining beasts fall away from him. He wasn't so lucky with the fourth; it launched itself upwards, faster than he could do anything to stop, and a taloned hand wrapped itself around the ankle of his bad leg and squeezed. The weight alone brought searing pain up the length of his body, and when the talons bit into him, scraping at bone, blackness gathered at the edges of his sight. He pointed the gun downward and let off three rounds, but his aim was off. He swung, left then right, banging hard into the cliff face both times. He was aware of Duffield shouting, somewhere above, but the pain drove every other thought from him, and all he could do was hang there as the talons at his ankle gripped ever tighter.

A single shot rang out, and he felt the round whistle past his nose. As suddenly as it had come the weight fell away from him as the dead beast plunged into the ravine.

But the pain stayed, and the blackness beckoned.

He gave himself to it.

-9-

They had gone twenty paces up the interior stairwell when Wiggo heard the distinctive pop-pop of gunfire from behind them, somewhere in the far distance outside.

I hope that's the bloody cavalry.

He considered retracing their steps, but that would mean dealing with the pack of beasts they'd left outside, and that would also mean using ammo that was already running dangerously low to his mind. Besides, the top of the pyramid had looked to be near the roof at its highest point; hearth and home was somewhere in that direction, and the longer they were still going up, the happier he would be. And if someone with modern weaponry was looking for them, up was also the obvious place for them to look. He trusted to that, and followed the others upward.

Ten steps later Wilkins called for a halt; they'd arrived on a wide landing at a three way junction. Stairwells went up on both the right and left hand sides of them, while the way ahead was a dark well, with steps leading deeper into the bowels of the pyramid. The dog strode over, looked down into the dark, and growled deep in its chest.

"That's good enough for me," Wiggo said. "We keep going up. Fifty-fifty choice, so let's go left, see if that gets us anywhere. If any fuckers show up, don't wait for an order. Put them down, hard and fast."

Wiggo was nearest to the left stairwell, so he took point, with Elsa and the dog at his back, Mac behind them and Wilkins at the rear. As he moved away from the deeper well going downwards he noted a change in the air; there was a definite animalistic odor rising up from the depths, and that in itself was more than enough to justify his decision to head upwards. But he only managed to go twelve steps before he reached another landing, this one rectangular, with upward passageways in all four walls.

"Fuck. It's a maze. I don't suppose anybody brought a ball of string?" he said, then turned to Elsa. "Time for some rules, lass, just in case you get lost."

He took his knife and scored an arrow on the wall just inside the leftmost passage.

"This means we went this way."

He traced an imaginary X at the rear of the arrow.

"If there's an X it means we went this way, and found fuck all. Got it?"

Elsa nodded.

"If lost, follow the arrows, and only arrows, it should lead us all to the same place," she said.

Wiggo nodded.

"And trust me, it's a system that works. Got me out of trouble a few times in the past."

Her head-light glared in his eyes as she moved and another thought struck him.

"How long will the batteries last?"

"I've been wondering that myself. A couple hours more, at the most?"

"That's what I thought. Best we get a move on then. I've no desire to be buggering about down here in the dark."

He led them all left and upward.

They went up, keeping left, through three more landings, with Wiggo scoring an arrow on the wall of each passageway. The passages were all the same; dry, slightly dusty, but with no sign of life whatsoever, not even moss, lichen or insect. The next leftward steps proved to be different.

The first sign was the smell, an acrid tang that burnt in the throat, the source of which was obvious when another turn brought Wiggo face to face with steps coated in clumps of pale droppings.

"Shit," Elsa said at his back.

"Yep," Wiggo replied. "And a whole fuckload of it at that. Stay here, I'll take a shufti."

He went gingerly up the steps, taking care not to step in the thicker piles of the crap. As before the stairwell led to a landing, but this was higher, more vaulted, and he didn't need his flashlight for the pyramid had collapsed inward here at some time distant and was open to the elements; open enough that the bats had got in. A clump of them were roosting, hanging from the ceiling near an opening, a dozen or more, tightly packed and swaying gently as if breathing in unison. There were three other passageways off the landing, but all of them looked to be partially clogged with even thicker piles of the pale crap.

Wiggo backed off, as quiet as he could manage, never taking his eyes from the roosting bats until he was safely back under cover of the stairwell. Elsa looked up at him as he descended, and he shook his head.

"There's no easy way up that way. Let's try another."

They went back to the landing and regrouped. Wiggo scored an X behind the arrow on the passageway wall, then brought them all up to speed on the bats and the situation above.

"We might find that the whole upper level is the same and infested with the buggers, in which case fighting our way up will be our only option. But let's not wake the beasts up if we don't have to. We go right."

-10-

Banks woke with thin, green-tinged light in his eyes and the taste of warm water at his lips. He was sitting up with his back to what felt like the bole of a tree, and Duffield was leaning over him. They were under a canopy of broad, rhubarb-like leaves on what appeared to be a forest of similar large plants. The ground underneath him felt pillow-soft and mossy.

"What happened?" he said, through dry, thick lips.

"I had to haul you up. No offence, Cap, but you need to go on a diet; nearly fucking killed me."

Banks looked down. His trouser leg was slit from ankle to knee, showing a fresh bandage below it.

"What's the damage?"

"Deep contusions from the new wounds," Duffield said, "but nothing life threatening. It's the old wound that has me worried."

"Aye, me too lad," Banks said, and winced as he tried to move and got a flare of fresh pain for his trouble.

"You need to rest, Cap," Duffield said.

"I need a whole fuckload of things," he replied. "But rest isn't an option. How long was I out?"

"Just long enough for me to patch you up," Duffield said. "I've got some morphine, if you think you can handle it?"

"Save it. I'll let you know if I need it. Any more gunfire? Or beasties?"

"No, to both."

Banks gritted his teeth, got his good leg under him, and tried to stand. His bad leg wasn't having any of it and immediately buckled. If Duffield hadn't caught him he'd have fallen in a heap. As it was he got lowered gently back against the bole.

"Like I said, Cap," Duffield said. "You need to rest."

"Rest and be damned. The lads are in trouble somewhere out there."

"Possibly so. But they're not the only ones. Your leg's fucked, Cap, that's the truth of it."

"Tell me something I don't know, lad. Give me some of that morphine, and see if you can find something I can use as a cane. We're moving out in ten minutes, fucked leg or no fucked leg."

The morphine kicked in quickly, and what with that, and a smoke, Banks felt quite light headed but pain free by the time Duffield returned. The lad dropped a long stick at Banks' side.

It looked like wood, but was more pliable, almost like a rod of hefty black rubber.

"These things look like a mixture of tree and rhubarb," Duffield said. "The old ones are more woody. I was able to hack that off of one. Will it do the job?"

"Only one way to find out," Banks replied, and got his good leg under him again. This time he rose with the help of the new stick, and was able to stand upright. The bad leg felt weak and unstable, but he was going to be able to get along on it, if he was careful...and the morphine kept doing its job.

He nodded towards Duffield.

"Good enough, for now. Any clue as to where we should be going?"

"There was more activity in the sky over to my right when I was foraging," the younger man replied. "That's probably our best bet."

"Then lay on, MacDuff. And don't spare the horses."

Banks hefted his pack onto his back, slung the rifle over his shoulder, and followed, hobbling as well as he was able, as Duffield set off under the canopy.

It was hard going, and would have been even without the gammy leg, but Duffield was doing most of the heavy work, tearing the more recalcitrant of the fleshy leaves away and out of their paths with sheer brute force and an energy that Banks could only dream of. The morphine was keeping the worst of the pain at bay but he felt as weak as a babe and every step was an act of sheer will and bloody-mindedness, the thought of the squad being in danger driving him when the will threatened to fade. By rights he should have been watching their back for any encroachment by the lizards, or anything else that might inhabit this place, but almost his entire focus was just on putting one foot in front of another.

He had managed twenty minutes in this fashion when Duffield turned, took one look at him, and called a halt.

"Shit, Cap, you look like death warmed up. Take five and have a smoke. You need it."

Banks slumped to the ground, his back once again against a bole. When he stretched his leg he felt the first twinge of returning pain.

A smoke helped, as did the enforced rest, but he wasn't looking forward to getting up again. Duffield must have seen it in his face.

"Look, Cap, I can go on ahead faster on my own, have a reccy. You stay here and rest; I've got this."

Banks was too tired to argue. Besides, the lad had a point. All he was doing was slowing the possible rescue down. He nodded, and lit a second cigarette from the butt of the first.

"Just don't forget about me, okay?" he said.

"I'll head on for fifteen minutes, tops, then come straight back. Just stay awake that long."

"With the pain that's coming on? That's not going to be my problem."

"There's more morphine…"

"No. Then I would be asleep, and I've got a feeling there might be things out there just waiting for that kind of opportunity. No, you get away and on, lad. I'll be here waiting when you get back."

They synchronized their watches.

"Half an hour, trust me," Duffield said. "And if I don't come back…"

"I'll come looking. Trust me," Banks replied, and gave Duffield a mock salute as the younger man-made his way off into the foliage.

Banks sat smoking, both the walking rod and his rifle in his lap, trying to empty his mind of its now many and various worries. He wasn't having much success, and was wishing he'd taken the offer of the morphine. The pain levels kept ramping up; it was as if his left leg was on fire one minute, and as if doused in ice the next, but both conditions were equally debilitating and he had to grit his teeth against a desperate scream that wanted to get out. No matter the position, whether sitting up or half-lying down, the pain just kept getting worse, until he was forced, shakily to his feet, leaning heavily on the stick and stomping back and forth in a small area, trying to loosen muscles that had gone hard as cold iron.

He checked his watch.

Only ten minutes?

It had felt like at least an hour. He leaned against the bole of one of the trees and lit another smoke. He had only taken one drag when there was a distinct rustle in the foliage. It had come from his right, and Duffield had departed to the left. Banks wasn't inclined to call out to check. He swung his rifle round and aimed in the direction of the sound.

It came again, this time from two yards further left. He tracked it with the barrel of the rifle.

Well, come on if you're coming, you bastarding thing.

Nothing appeared out of the foliage, but there was a second sound, this time directly to his right, a snuffle, as if something sniffing the air, followed by a low hiss. An answering hiss came from his left, then another from behind the tree he was leaning against. He was surrounded, and didn't have to see them to know that the lizard beasts had once again found him.

He only had two options open to him, and fleeing on foot wasn't one of them; he could either spray the area with bullets and hope for the best, or he could try to buy time and hope that Duffield might come to his rescue. He didn't like his chances much either way, but playing for time seemed the least risky of the two.

He turned to face the tree and looked up; the branches diverged into the canopy some six feet above his head. The outer surface of the trunk was tough and ridged and he thought he could climb it.

But if I can, so can they.

He stopped trying to second guess himself when another hiss, louder this time, came from his right and the foliage rustled. He stowed his rifle at his back, slid the walking stick through the harness on his jacket, hoping it would stay in place, and began to climb, as fast as he could manage without having to put weight on the bad leg.

He was two feet from where he could pull himself up into the canopy when two of the lizard things came out of the foliage and, sniffing like dogs on a scent, approached the base of the tree.

"I hope you're on your way back, lad," he muttered. "Looks like I'm going to need some help here."

He dragged his weary body up into a forked hollow in the branches where the canopy opened out; it was as high as he was going to be able to go. He looked down.

The first of the beasts was already starting to climb.

Any time now would be fine, lad. Any time now.

-11-

They tried six different routes upward in the pyramid. Of those, four led to various entrances to the open chamber where the bats were roosting, and two led to complete dead ends of an empty room with no other entrances. Now they were back at the first junction standing above the steps that led even deeper down. Wiggo was left with a dilemma; either go down into the darker bowels of the place, or try to sneak past the roosting bats and head further up. Neither option was appealing.

The thing that decided for him was the fact that the headlights they wore were showing signs of weakening; the batteries hadn't gone yet, but they were going. At least if they went the bats route they'd have some natural light.

And we'll still be going up.

Once he made his mind up he wasted no more time thinking about it.

"This is going to be tricky," he said to the others. "We're going to have to move fast, but quietly, and hope for some luck. But as far as I can see it's our best hope right now."

He turned to Elsa.

"Can you keep Danny quiet? On previous behavior he's going to want to at least growl at the beasts, and we can't have that."

"He'll do what he's told," Elsa replied. "He's a good dog."

Danny's tail wagged enthusiastically in agreement, and Wiggo could only smile.

"Okay then. We go up. And try not to trample in too much of the bat shite; it's murder on the carpets."

Wiggo took point again and went leftward up the flights of stairs at trouble time until he reached the point where he could smell the acrid odor and see faint light from up ahead. He switched off his head-light, and silently motioned for the others to do the same. Elsa bent to Danny and looked the dog in the eye.

"Keep quiet, boy. Quiet."

Danny's tail wagged slowly, then he moved to stand tight by Elsa's knee. The woman looked up at Wiggo and mouthed one word.

"Ready."

Wiggo again avoided the worst of the droppings and stepped quickly up and into the chamber. He didn't hear the others at his back. He took that as a good sign.

A quick glance upward showed that the group of bats were still roosting there, and still swaying together as if collectively taking breath. There was no trace of wind, no sound but his own breathing. He breathed through his mouth to try to minimize the smell but it tickled at his tonsils and he had to stifle a cough. Even then the soft sound sounded much too loud in the quiet chamber, and when he looked up a shiver ran through the group of bats, as if the cough had indeed been noted, but disregarded as not important enough to investigate.

He took another step forward. The crap covered the floor completely here and there was no way to ignore it; he could only hope he wasn't ruining what was a perfectly good pair of boots. It also meant that every step brought another wave of acrid odor up from the floor; if the bats' sense of smell was as good as their hearing, there was going to be trouble.

Wiggo set his gaze on the upward stairwell to his right; it looked to have slightly less of a shite-coat than the others. He headed, slowly, in that direction, one eye on the stairwell, the other on the bats above. He got halfway across the room before the plan went sideways on him.

Something shifted in the darkness of his target stairwell, something low and sinuous. It was joined by another, and now two of the lizard beasts were on the steps, not coming forward into the chamber, but most definitely blocking any way up.

The only way to get past them was by shooting them; but that would wake the bats.

And when Wiggo looked at the other possible stairwells there were lizards occupying them too; the largest they'd seen so far, looking to be almost ten feet from nose to tail, heads the size of that of a horse, two to each stairwell, gazes fixed on Wiggo, not coming forward, but most definitely, and deliberately, blocking any way further up.

Wiggo turned to the others and motioned for them to go back the way they had come. As they retreated to the original stairwell, so too did the lizards come on, softly and silently across the floor of the chamber, as if they too knew not to disturb the bats at roost.

Wiggo was the last of the group to retreat into the stairwell. By then eight lizards crawled slowly through the chamber under the roosting bats.

"Let's see how you like it," Wiggo said, raised his pistol and fired a single shot in the general direction of the bats.

The result was immediate; the bats, as one, fell from the ceiling as if a switch had been pulled, and launched immediately into a dive, making straight for the lizards. The lizards got in each others' way in an attempt to scurry for cover, and then it was too late. The bats fell on them, teeth and talons tearing. The air was immediately filled with screams and howls and high washes of blood spray as the chamber resolved into a charnel pit of violence and feeding frenzy of bats eating lizards and lizards eating bats and neither giving any quarter. Wiggo added to it by putting another bullet in the head of a lizard coming his way in an attempt to escape, then quickly turned back to the others.

"Let's get out of here before we get put on the menu," he said, and once again led the way, having to put on his head-light as they reached the darker depths of the stairwell.

A minute later they were back where they had started, in the four-way chamber where the dark well led down into the depths. Danny took one look at it and growled again, deep in his chest.

"Aye, I hear you, boy," Wiggo said. "I don't like it much myself."

He turned to the others.

"We can't get up, and I'm not keen on fucking about down in the dark there. My initial thought is to find another way…go back out onto the Yellow Brick Road and follow it to the other end. What do you say?"

"Just as long as I get to be Dorothy, I'm in, Sarge," Wilkins said, and dropped him a wink.

At least morale isn't a problem. Yet.

Mac nodded in agreement with Wiggo. Elsa hadn't yet answered. She was looking down the well, a puzzled expression on her face.

"Something?" Wiggo asked.

"Maybe," she said. "But I'd feel better talking about it outside."

Wiggo gave her a mock salute.

"Outside it is then. Mac, you take point."

Mac turned away, then back again immediately.

"We've got a problem here, Sarge," he said, keeping his voice low. Wiggo saw what he meant as soon as he too turned around. He looked down the steps towards the main entrance of the pyramid to see ranks of the lizards blocking any possible escape; there appeared to be at least twenty of them, all big buggers like the ones they'd just seen in the bat roost. They weren't moving, just sitting there, eyes fixed on Wiggo and the others. Danny growled again until Elsa put a hand on his flanks.

Wilkins spoke up.

"They're over here now too, Sarge," he said. Wiggo looked over in that direction and saw that the other stairwells now also had a pair of lizards blocking any way out in that direction.

We're being herded like fucking sheep.

As if to prove the point, the group of beasts on the steps outside began to crawl upwards towards them.

-12-

Banks took careful aim from his position in the forked branches of the tree, aimed between the climbing beast's eyes, and put a single bullet in its head. It fell away and was immediately pounced on by three others who tore at it as if they were ravenous. A fourth, however, was showing more interest in Banks than in fresh meat and it came at the tree at a run, taking a leap that was going to bring it perilously close to him. He put two rounds in its exposed throat and belly. Its dead weight shook the tree as it hit the bole, almost toppling Banks out of the branches and sending a fresh jarring flare of pain up his leg. The dead thing fell in a heap right on top of where the others were feeding and was immediately incorporated in the feast.

Banks had trouble focusing. Blackness crept in at the edges of his sight again, threatening to throw him down into unconsciousness. He knew that he'd be a goner within seconds if that happened, and shook his head, hard, trying to maintain concentration as another of the beasts showed signs of paying him some attention.

Come on, lad. Where are you? You must have heard the shots.

His silent plea was answered almost immediately. He lined up another shot, but the target fell away as Duffield stepped into view and immediately sent a volley of rounds into the pack of beasts, then walked forward and calmly and with a single shot for each, delivered the coup-de-grace to any that were still showing signs of life.

The lieutenant looked up at Banks.

"Sorry I'm late, Cap. Came as fast as I could. Any more of these buggers about that I should be aware of?"

"None that I've seen," Banks replied. He got himself turned around enough to dangle from the thickest branch, but if he dropped from there he was going to do even more damage to his leg. "I could do with a hand here though."

Between the two of them they managed to manhandle Banks down out of the tree, but not before he took another jarring jolt on the bad leg. Duffield held him up as they limped away from the carnage and found a clearer area some twenty yards distant. Banks slumped down with his back to the bole of another tree, and didn't complain when Duffield administered a dose of morphine, a drink of water, and another smoke.

"Thanks for the rescue," he said.

"Looked like you were doing okay on your own to me, Cap," Duffield said, "but anyway, it's all part of the service. And my wee jaunt wasn't a waste. I've found them; or at least, I think I've found where they are."

"Tell me."

"There's a roadway, only five minutes away. It leads to yon pyramid we saw from the high window. And while I was having a gander at it I heard a shot. Just the one, but it was a shot. I think, if they're anywhere, they're in yon pyramid."

The morphine kicked in while Banks was finishing his smoke. He didn't hang about wasting its effect, but, using the black stick, pushed himself upright, almost overbalancing until he got his good leg under him properly. Duffield looked at him, an eyebrow raised.

"Don't give me any lip, lad," Banks said. "I'm not in the best of moods. Get me to this road while I'm still able to walk."

Once again Duffield blazed the trail. The foliage wasn't as thick here which made the going easier, and Banks was now more proficient with the stick, falling into a rhythm that put the least pressure on the wounded leg. With that, and the continuing effect of the morphine, he was pleasantly surprised to still be feeling relatively okay when they emerged out of the forest and onto an ancient cobbled walkway. His heart fell when he looked along the road to see that their destination, the black pyramid, was still a mile or more ahead of them.

At least they had the road to themselves; nothing moved, not even a breath of wind. The air was still, smelling slightly of old smoke, and if any of the lizards were still stalking them they were staying out of sight, hopefully wary of launching an attack after the carnage Duffield's volley fire had wrought on the others of their kind. Nor was there any sign of anything flying in the sky, neither above them or above the pyramid itself.

Without allowing himself a pause to rest, he set off along the roadway at a lurch, with Duffield at his side.

"I'm pretty glad to have brought you along, lad," he said. "In case you haven't noticed, you're doing just fine."

Duffield laughed, and waved a hand around the scene.

"Fine isn't the word I had in mind. Is it usually this freaky in your team?"

It was Banks' turn to laugh.

"Naw. It's usually worse."

While they walked Banks took his mind off his aches and pains by recounting one of their more wild exploits, the tale of the sea serpent in the North Sea that both was, and wasn't a real sea serpent after all. It was while telling that he remembered it had been Wiggo's first real test of his own initiative. He'd come through that one with flying colors.

I hope he's doing at least as well this time.

He was surprised to look up some time later to see that the pyramid was much nearer. Something on the cobbles caught his eye, and when he had a closer look he saw it was all too familiar; a cigarette butt crushed underfoot by a heavy boot.

"We're finally on the right track at least; they definitely came this way."

Duffield didn't answer and when Banks looked over the lad wasn't looking at the ground or the pyramid, but up towards the roof.

"What do you think that is, Cap?"

It was a darker mass on the stone, and appeared to be constantly in movement, shifting as if in a breeze. Banks remembered the black things he'd seen in the air when looking out the high window, and a cold finger of dread ran down his spine.

"Trouble, lad. That's what it is. Let's get along before it finds us."

When he took a first lurch forward he felt a twinge of pain in the wounded leg; the morphine was wearing off, and much too soon at that. His leg threatened to buckle. He forced it into submission and kept moving.

Not now. Not when we're so close.

He gritted his teeth as the pain got exponentially more severe with every step.

-13-

"What do we do, Sarge?" Mac asked in a whisper. "Fight our way out?"

The lizards continued to creep upwards. There were more of them than Wiggo had originally thought, and he stopped counting at thirty when he saw there were at least as many again coming up at the rear from out on the road. If they had their rifles he might have made a stand, but with only the handguns they didn't have the firepower to hold a line against a full on attack from the beasts.

"No. We'd be overrun in seconds. We've got no choice. We have to retreat."

The trouble with that was that their only route to possible safety was now down into the dark well, the very place where the beasts wanted them to go.

What other choice do I have?

And the longer he took to make a decision, the more time the beasts would have to close in around them.

"Fuck it. If we can't go up, we go down. Wilkins, Mac, watch my back. Elsa… you're with me."

At first it seemed that Danny wasn't going to follow. The hairs on the dog's neck rose, and it growled loudly, baring its teeth, but when Elsa took two steps down into the dark he was at her heel, following, obedient, but still growling softly.

Wiggo took the lead and went down the steps. There was an odor here too, but not like the acrid tang of the bat shit. This was thicker, meatier somehow, much more animalistic in nature. And the walls on either side of them were no longer just dry stone. Pallid gray lichens hung from the roof and translucent, faintly luminescent mosses clambered in mosaic patterns on all the old stonework. The further they descended, the more mosses they encountered, and the lighter the passageway became. By twenty steps down Wiggo was able to switch off the head-light.

At least that's one fucking thing I don't have to worry about for a while.

Mac spoke from the steps above him.

"The beasties have stopped up on the landing. They're not following."

Two for two. I wish I could believe things are looking up.

He went down ten more steps. The odor had strengthened, and there was even more light coming from below, along with a sense of space and emptiness, a trace of an echo in the air. His hunch that they were approaching an opening was proved right a few steps later, although it was more than just an opening.

He came off the bottom step into a huge cathedral-like chamber. The whole area was full of glistening light extruded by luminescent mosses that gave off a shimmering, almost rainbow-like aurora that hung high above. The floor of the chamber was dominated by two things.

The first was a pale serpent lying in the center of the chamber, coiled in on itself, each coil eight feet high. He estimated its total length from sharp nose to forked tail at somewhere over sixty feet, and its head looked to be the size of a pickup truck. The scaled body rippled and mirrored the dancing aurora, and its eyelids, currently closed, flickered and shimmered as if it dreamed where it lay. The other thing of note in the chamber was what the serpent was lying among… a scattered profusion of opalescent, flattened oval, objects each three feet from end to end. They were obviously eggs, and there were over a hundred of them that Wiggo could see. Scattered fragments of broken shell and old bones strewn among them completed the picture.

That was what he could see. What he couldn't see were any other exits. The only way out of the chamber was the way they had come in. He was still mulling over the implications when Elsa leaned over and whispered in his ear.

"I was right."

"Right about what, lass?"

"All the beasts we've been seeing are suffering from malnutrition. They're literally starving. Look at her. Just look."

Now that she had mentioned it, he knew what to search for, and saw it immediately; the rib-cage of the great worm showed sharply against its torso, and the muscles stood out proudly on its great thighs, stretching the scales and the skin beneath tight to almost splitting point. There was not an ounce of fat anywhere on the beast. It looked worse than starved; it looked skeletal.

Elsa whispered again.

"Something… maybe the fire…disrupted the ecosystem down here so badly that it hasn't recovered. And these beasts are paying the price. It's probably why they started appearing up above; they're getting desperate for food."

"I ken how they feel," Wiggo replied. "That's another problem solved, then. But it doesn't help us any."

Another thought struck him.

"I was right too. We were herded down here, weren't we?"

"It certainly looks like it."

"So we're what's for supper?"

She didn't reply. She didn't have to, for it was the obvious answer.

"We can't wait for her to wake up," he said.

"I don't think it's her we need to worry about right now," Elsa replied, and pointed to one of the nearest eggs just as a crack ran from the more pointed end down to the base, the sound echoing around the chamber.

As if on cue, more cracks rose up and all around the room the eggs started to shift and rock slightly from side to side.

"Marines, we are leaving," Wiggo muttered, and stepped back towards the stairs. But they were caught between the beasts above and the threat below, with nowhere to run, nowhere to hide. If there was a cavalry charge coming to their rescue, he only hoped it would be soon.

Another batch of eggs cracked, and the mother of them all stirred in her sleep, her tail swishing gently from side to side.

Any time now would be good for me, lads.

-14-

The rest of the walk along the road to the pyramid became a race between Banks' increasing pain and his ability to keep moving despite it. By the time they were on close approach to the steps up to the entrance he was willing to call it a draw. He was forced into rest only by the sight of a pack of the low lizard beasts congregated at the top of the steps. They hadn't taken note of the two men yet, seeming to be intent on keeping a watch on something inside the pyramid itself, but it was surely only going to be a matter of time.

The only other things of note were two carcasses of winged beasts at the foot of the steps; they had been mostly devoured and torn asunder, thus hard to identify, but looked like some kind of large bats, albeit ones with dog-like heads and too many limbs. Banks guessed this was what was roosting in the roof above. Looking at the remains, then at the beasts in the entranceway, he began to get an idea.

"We need to get inside," he said, having to speak through gritted teeth against the pain. "And we need a diversion, but I doubt you're going to like it."

"So what else is new?" Duffield said, smiling. "I'm up for it, whatever it is."

Banks pointed up at the roof.

"We need to get those things up there to come down here. And I'm planning on using you as bait."

Duffield's smile never slipped.

"You're right, Cap. I don't like it. Where do you need me?"

"Here, on the road, and on my signal make some noise so that yon pack of beasties at the entrance see you. I'll be under the canopy, watching your back."

"And the flying things?"

"I'll get their attention, you get the beasties' attention, and then we see what happens when the two of them get together. I'm hoping they'll take to eating each other, and we'll be able to slip up the steps while they're busy."

"And if they're good pals and decide to gang up on us?"

"Then we're royally fucked," Banks replied and kicked at the carcasses. "But I'm hoping these tell a different story. And unless you've got any better ideas…?"

"Nothing that immediately springs to mind."

"Then just stay there and look like food," Banks said, slipping away under the nearest large tree then aiming his rifle up towards where the bats were roosting. "The shit's about to hit the fan."

Banks fired a shot upward and the bats obliged; the clump broke apart and the beasts launched into a diving attack. At the same moment Duffield put his fingers to his lips and whistled, as if calling a dog. Up on the pyramid steps the beasts took note, wheeled as one, and launched forward; they too headed directly for the lieutenant.

"What now?" Duffield shouted.

"Hide, ya big daft bugger. Get under cover."

Duffield leapt under the canopy just as the first of the bats and the lead of the lizards met in the space where he had been a second before. The roadway turned into roiling chaos and mayhem as the lizards and bats tore and chewed at each other in feeding frenzy. Duffield crept forward and tapped Banks on the shoulder, pointing towards the pyramid; their way was, for the moment, clear.

Banks swayed, almost toppled, trying to push himself upright, but waved away Duffield's concern. With the stick in one hand and his rifle in the other he lurched along the roadside at the edge of the canopy. He prayed under his breath that neither bat nor lizard would take notice, for all he had energy for at that moment was putting one foot in front of the other.

The feeding frenzy continued behind them, the air full of screeching, hissing and the flapping of leathery wings which sounded like drying sheets in a stiff breeze. Banks refused to look back, keeping his gaze firmly on the steps ahead. The black opening at the top of them gaped like a mouth ready to receive food as Duffield, with Banks only a step behind, reached the bottom of the stairs. Duffield stepped up, and Banks attempted to follow, but his legs rebelled, and went weak under him. He fell forward, saved only from smacking his face on stone by Duffield's quick thinking and helping hand. Banks was quickly back upright, but his legs refused point blank to take any steps upward.

"Fuck," he muttered under his breath.

"No worries. I've got you, Cap," Duffield said, and before Banks could complain, the lieutenant scooped him up in a fireman's lift and was going up the steps at a fast trot, with as little effort as he might if carrying a baby.

"Remind me never to fuck with you, lad," Banks said as he was lowered to his feet in the entrance.

Down below on the roadway the melee continued, but some of the bats were spiraling up and away, and the lizards had the upper hand over the survivors on the ground. It was more of a feast than a battle now, but if it meant they kept ignoring him and Duffield, Banks was okay with either.

He turned and looked into the depths of the pyramid.

"More bloody stairs," he muttered, and his leg flared in pain in agreement, almost causing him to stumble again. "I'm not going to get very far like this. Any more of that morphine going?"

"I don't think you should take more, Cap. It's as liable to knock you out on your arse as to be of any help with walking."

"I'll take the chance," Banks replied. "It's either that or you carry me about like a fucking ventriloquist's dummy, and I don't think either of us could take that for long. Morphine, lad, and be quick about it. The way yon lizards are eating, they'll be ready for seconds before too long."

Duffield administered an injection into the meat of Banks' thigh, then showed him an empty vial.

"That's your lot, Cap. The return journey's going to be rough on you."

"I'll deal with that when the time comes. Let's find the others first, and see what later brings."

Three gunshots sounded, one right after the other from deep in the bowels of the pyramid.

"Found them," Duffield said, but Banks was already on the move.

-15-

The nearest egg to Wiggo rocked too far to one side and toppled over, two new cracks appearing in the surface. A tear formed, and a thin talon emerged, working at the new hole slowly, almost feebly, trying to open the shell from the inside. Again, as if a silent cue had been passed, eggs all over the hall exhibited similar behavior and the sound of cracking and tearing shells filled the chamber. The mother serpent stirred, her main coils loosening and tightening again, and her eye movements under the lids became more rapid and fluttery.

I do not want to be anywhere near here if she wakes up.

"Stay here with the lads," Wiggo said to Elsa. "I'm going back up to have a shufti. We need to find a way out of here. And soon."

When he started back up the steps, Danny came with him at his knee, nose raised high as if checking for trouble. The dog growled softly deep in its chest.

"Aye, lad. I'm none too happy about it either," Wiggo said softly. "But needs must."

He only got four steps before he was stopped by a sharp hiss from above him that was immediately taken up by several others in accompaniment. He looked up and saw four pairs of eyes staring back at him, four pale bodies barely visible in the gloom. They weren't coming forward, but they weren't backing off. As before it looked like the beasts had the squad where they wanted them; fresh meat on the bone for the new hatchlings.

"Aye, like that's going to be happening any time soon," Wilkins muttered. He raised his pistol, taking aim, to see if it got any reaction. It got a sharp hiss from the beasts… and a loud bark from Danny. Without warning the dog launched itself up the steps, heading straight for the beasts.

"Down, boy, heel," Wiggo shouted, but far too late. The dog was already among the beasts in a raul of gnashing teeth and flailing limbs.

"Fuck this," Wiggo said, and stepped up quickly, weapon raised. He had to take careful aim, and only got one really clear line of sight. He put two bullets into the largest of the beasts; one in the throat, one in the head, and it went down hard. One of the others stopped harrying the dog and took to frenzied feeding on the new carcass. He put a round in that one's head too, just as Danny yelped in pain and blood flew.

"Hold on, boy," Wiggo said. "I'm here."

He couldn't get another shot without possibly hitting the dog, so did the only thing he could think of at the time; he holstered the pistol, stepped up, and, two-handed, grabbed at one of the beast's tails, and dragged it bodily out of the fray, using his weight to start a hammer-thrower's swing. The muscles of his lower back screamed in pain and the beast squealed in anger, even as he swung its head straight into the passageway wall where it smashed like a breaking egg.

Wiggo dropped the tail and turned to see that Danny was cornered into a rough alcove, teeth bared, as a beast loomed above it ready to strike. He reached for his gun, his heart sinking as he saw he was going to be too late, when two shots rang out and the beast fell away down the steps. He looked after it, expecting to see Wilkins or Mac, but there was nobody down there. A well known voice spoke from above them.

"Aye, it's me, lad. Here to save your arse. Again."

Wiggo turned, just in time to catch his captain as the man's legs gave way beneath him and he fell in a faint, a dead weight in Wiggo's arms.

Another voice spoke from up the steps.

"Friendly, coming in," it said, and a younger man appeared in view. "Duffield," the newcomer said, and pointed at the unconscious captain. "I'm wi' him."

The newcomer helped Wiggo lower the captain to the ground.

"What happened to him?" Wiggo said.

"His bad leg, and too much hurry," Duffield said.

"Aye. That would do it," Wiggo muttered. "But thanks for coming anyway."

"Where's the others?"

Wiggo motioned.

"Down below. I'll fetch them. But I've got another pal to see to first."

He was pleased to see that Danny was already walking, albeit unsteadily, out of the alcove. The dog had a bleeding wound at its neck, but it didn't look too deep, and wasn't slowing it down as it stepped down to the closest dead beast, lifted a leg, and pissed on the body.

"Good lad," Wiggo said, and Danny's tail wagged enthusiastically as it came to heel.

Wiggo looked down at Banks' unconscious body.

"Get the others," Duffield said, "I've got the captain."

"Who died and made you boss, son?" Wiggo said.

"That's Lieutenant son, to you, Sergeant," the newcomer replied. "But I'm not pulling rank here. I'm just asking you to shift your lardy arse; in case you haven't noticed, fresh meat's at a premium here; I'm guessing these dead fuckers are going to be attracting attention any second now."

"From above and below," Wiggo muttered, and threw Duffield a mock salute. "Aye, aye, sir. Here I go, shifting my lardy arse."

He met the others at the foot of the steps; they were already backing away from the main chamber, the two soldiers guarding Elsa as they stepped away from where several hatchlings crawled, seemingly blindly, on the rough floor.

"Marines, we are leaving," Wiggo said.

"We heard shots," Wilkins said. "Trouble?"

"Dealt with," Wiggo said. "For now. And the cavalry's here; two of them anyway."

He said no more, afraid of wasting time. Over Wilkins' shoulder he saw that the great serpent was uncoiling, shifting its weight as if in preparation to move.

"Up, and quick," he said. "The sooner we're out of here the better I'll feel."

Elsa had bent to check on Danny.

"He's hurt."

"Aye," Wiggo said. "But you should see the other guy." He took her by the shoulder and lifted her up. "Now come on. He can walk just fine. That's more than can be said of my captain, and I need to see to him. So come if you're coming."

Something shifted in the center of the chamber, rocks and stones moving. Wiggo looked over and met a huge eye the size of a dinner plate, open and staring right at him.

The serpent raised its snout and let out a hissing wail like a scalded cat. It was answered from somewhere else in the bowels of the structure by a chorus of wails, a high cacophony of a choir of beasts in pain.

"Time to go," Wiggo said, and took to the stairs, with Elsa and Danny right behind him and Wilkins and Mac covering their retreat.

-16-

Banks woke slowly. The last thing he remembered was a headlong rush down a flight of steps, seeing Wiggo, then shooting one of the beasts. But it wasn't Wiggo that leaned over him now, it was young Duffield, concern writ large on his face.

"For fuck's sake, Cap, don't do that again. You had me worried."

He was lying on cold stone, and his bad leg refused to comply when he ordered it to help him get up. He was half-lifted, half climbing as he stood, unsteadily, leaning against the younger man.

"Wiggo and the others?" he said.

"We're here, Cap," Wiggo said, coming into view from below. He had a woman and a dog with him, and the other two squaddies at the rear. "Introductions will have to wait. We've got more trouble at our backs. We should go."

Banks tried to take a step. His bad leg again refused to comply. Duffield got him fully upright and bore most of the weight.

"I've got him, Sergeant. You lead. We'll be right behind you."

Wiggo looked to Banks for confirmation. Banks nodded.

"The lad here's been taking care of me just fine so far. If he says he's got me, he's got me. Don't worry about me; get us the fuck out of here while I'm still standing."

Even with Duffield taking the weight, and with at least some morphine still in his system, pain gripped like a vise in his leg, threatening to throw him into unconsciousness again with every step. He felt half-dead by the time they came up out of the pyramid into the light, but there was no time to slow; a commotion had been slowly building at their backs, high, hissing howls in the depths of the pyramid, getting ever louder. Fine dust shook from the roof and the whole structure trembled, as if something massive was on the move inside.

"Mammie's awake, and I don't think she's all that happy about it," Wiggo said. "If you've got a plan of escape, Cap, we should start now."

Duffield answered for him.

"We came over the ravine the same way you did. We should go back that way."

"There's no bridge over yon chasm though," Wiggo said.

"We brought ropes," Duffield replied. "And left them there. We'll manage."

The noise from inside the pyramid went up a notch.

"I guess we will at that," Wiggo said. "We'll have to. Which way?"

Banks handed Wiggo his rifle, and pointed to the left.

"Over yonder, through the greenery, fast as you can. I'll be right behind you."

Wiggo led away down off the pyramid, with the woman, the dog, Wilkins and Mac following. Duffield helped Banks hobble down onto level ground. Banks tried a few steps using the black rubbery cane as support and nodded.

"I can manage, for a bit at least," he said, managing a thin smile although the pain was almost crippling. "Looks like you and I are watching the back. Don't let us fall too far behind, lad."

"You need to rest, Cap, and soon."

"Then get me home. All the rest I'll ever need is waiting for me there."

Wiggo and the others had already disappeared into the greenery. The foot of the pyramid was awash with corpses of both dead beasts and dead bats. High overhead, more of the bats circled but were showing no signs of launching a dive attack. Banks thought the main danger was probably going to come from inside the pyramid itself, given the rising cacophony of howling and hissing rising from the depths, and was proved right a second later when the entranceway filled with swarming, scuttling beasts.

The whole pyramid shook and trembled. The beasts crept forward into the light as stonework crumbled around them.

"No, thanks," Duffield said. "Not today."

He sent a volley of shots up to the entrance. Two of the beasts went down. The others leapt on the carcasses to feed.

"That should keep them busy," Duffield said.

"I'd say they're the least of our problems," Banks replied dryly as the top of the pyramid fell in on itself and a huge head the size of a pickup truck emerged, blinking, out of the rubble.

Banks didn't wait to see if Duffield would follow. He headed into the forest at the spot where the others had gone, head down and hirpling as fast as his pain and immobility would allow.

It wasn't going to allow him to go at any great haste, that much became obvious very quickly. And every step was more of a forward lurch then readjustment rather than a smooth pace, bringing jarring pain every time either foot touched ground. He clenched his teeth and persisted, but knew that it was now only the morphine that was keeping him going. Once that wore off, there would only be pain, and probably more of it than he could endure. He pushed the thought away; the squad were headed for safety, and there was still a chance for him to get there alongside. As long as that chance existed, he'd walk, even if he wore his feet down to stumps in the process.

-17-

The flight through the fleshy forest seemed to go on forever, and Wiggo knew that fatigue and hunger was going to become a real issue sooner rather than later. The only good thing was that there had been no sign of any attack, either from the lizards or the bats. Looking up, all that could be seen was the hanging canopy of leaves, and nothing moved in the undergrowth as they hurried through it.

They were heading, as far as he could tell, on a rough track that should, with a great deal of luck, lead them to the ravine. Whether it was the correct path or not, only time would tell, but at least they were making good progress. Elsa was keeping pace with him, and Danny seemed none the worse for wear from the neck wound which appeared to have stopped bleeding. Wiggo looked back and saw Wilkins and Mac only a few yards at their rear. There was no sign of the Cap or the young lieutenant, but Wiggo knew better than to stop and wait for them; the Cap would have his balls in a basket if there was any sign of slacking. Besides, he hadn't heard any gunfire; he took that to be a good sign that the Cap was still behind them, somewhere.

He slowed only long enough to light up a smoke. Elsa spoke at his side.

"This whole ecosystem is on the edge of collapse," she said.

"That's good, isn't it? All those lizard fuckers die off, there won't be any more problems up top. Everybody wins."

"I think, what did you call her, Mammie?... I think she might have something to say."

"Looked to me like she grew inside yon pyramid, or they put it up around her... she's going nowhere."

Even as he said it he didn't believe it; the squad were never that lucky for one thing, and for another he'd seen the sheer sense of strength and power of the serpent. The further he got from it, the better he'd feel. He was about to tell Elsa that when the view ahead opened up and seconds later he stood on the lip of the chasm. Looking to his right he was amazed to see a rope dangling from the cliff, and another on the opposite bank; maybe their luck was better than he imagined.

As he headed that way, Mac and Wilkins came up to join him and a minute later they all stood looking over the gorge. The rope hung, almost at their feet, tethered to one of the fleshy trees. Opposite them another rope hung down the far side, tethered to what looked like one of the remaining foundations of the now collapsed bridge. Wiggo looked down the length of rope to the chasm floor below. There were beasts down there, not all of them dead. A feast was still ongoing on a dozen or more carcasses, with seven, maybe eight of the large lizards gorging on the flesh...and blocking the only escape route.

"I could shimmy down there," Mac said. "You've got the rifle. You can cover me."

"And say you manage to get down quietly, and creep past the beasties. Say you even manage to drag yourself up the other side. Then, just for shits and giggles, say the beasts from over there come at you and you've only got your handgun? Then what do we do?" Wiggo asked.

The dilemma was solved by the arrival of Duffield. He had the Cap with him, not at his side, but slung over his shoulder in a fireman's lift. The younger man was red in the face, but hardly out of breath, and put Banks down slowly and gently with as little effort as he would expend putting a baby to bed.

"Don't mess with this one, lads," Banks said to them. "He's a tank in disguise." The captain was pale as a sheet and haggard with the pain, but his eyes were clear enough as he addressed Wiggo.

"Why haven't you started over, lad?"

Wiggo pointed down into the chasm.

"We've got a wee beastie problem. It's not a tank we need, it's a fucking climbing monkey."

"Luckily we brought one of them too," Duffield said. He removed the last of the coils of rope from its clip at his back and slung it over a shoulder, then handed his rifle to Wilkins.

"Cover me. This won't take long."

"You'll be alone on the far side for too long. And we can't all go down and back up," Wiggo said. "The captain for one won't make it."

Duffield winked.

"Trust me, Sarge. I've got a cunning plan."

"That's all we need," Wiggo replied. "Another fucking joker."

Duffield didn't reply. He was already over the edge and hooking his harness up to the rope.

"Remember to cover me. I'll need a minute on the bottom."

"You need a skelp on the bottom," Wiggo replied, and laughed, "But you'll get your minute. Now get going, time's a' wasting."

"Yes, sir," Duffield replied, and kicked away from the face, abseiling off and down so quickly that Wiggo thought he would do himself a mischief on hitting bottom.

Wiggo joined Wilkins in providing cover as Duffield touched down as gracefully as a dancer. Instead of making for the far side he started to tie the rope he'd taken with him to the dangling line.

"What the hell's he playing at?" Wiggo said.

"I've got an idea," Wilkins replied. "Just watch."

Duffield's luck held long enough for him to tie up one end of the rope. Still holding the coil he began to walk slowly across the bottom of the chasm, letting out rope as he went. Finally Wiggo saw his plan.

"Smart wee bugger. He's making a bridge."

"Aye," Wilkins replied. "If he gets the time. Look. To the left."

One of the beasts had raised its head from feeding and was now eyeing up Duffield, as if calculating the benefit of going after him instead of the feast in front of it. Duffield saw it too, but kept moving. He'd almost reached the dangling rope on the far side when the beast made its choice and left the carcass to make for fresher food. Duffield saw it coming but chose to ignore it, choosing instead to start climbing hand over hand up the far side rope, all the while still also holding the end of the free hanging rope he'd tied on.

The beast launched into a gallop.

Wilkins and Wiggo shot at the same time and the lizard fell in a heap. Duffield kept climbing, as if he didn't have a care in the world.

"He's got a cool head on his shoulders, I'll give him that," Wiggo said.

"I think the lad's going to surprise all of us," Banks said at his back. The captain was upright, and leaning on a cane, although he looked like he might collapse at any moment.

Only a minute later Duffield climbed up onto the far side, dragging the rope up with him and then tying the pieces together. He then looped it over the remnant of the foundation, found a rock, tied it to the end of the rope and shouted out.

"Incoming."

The rock flew straight and true and landed with a thud at Wiggo's feet. Wilkins looped it around the same tree as the fastened end and seconds later they had their makeshift bridge; two lengths of rope spanning the chasm. Duffield clambered back over to their side as easily as if he was taking a stroll down a pavement, feet on one rope, one hand on the other.

"Piece of piss," he said. "Even if I do say so myself."

"I'll let you know once we get everybody… and the dog… across in one piece," Wiggo replied, but couldn't help but be impressed by the younger man's attitude and demeanor.

It was immediately obvious that the main impediments to the plan would be getting Danny and Banks across to the other side. Wiggo had his doubts about Elsa but, although she kept her gaze firmly fixed on the far side all the time, she went over almost as swiftly as Duffield had managed. Soon they had Wilkins, Mac and Elsa over on the far side providing cover.

"Get the dog over," Banks said. "Our luck can only hold for so long."

As if to prove the point a now familiar high, hissing wail cut through the air, followed by a chorus of replies, as if the forest was suddenly alive and full of ravenous beasts.

Duffield again took the initiative, scooped up Danny over one shoulder and scampered easily across the rope using just one hand for balance.

Wiggo looked at Banks, then at the rope bridge, and back again.

"Yon leg won't hold you, Cap. You ken that."

"Well you're not leaving me here, so fuck off with that idea," Banks said, smiling through obvious pain.

Duffield made another journey back across and addressed Wiggo.

"I can take him."

"Don't be daft man; the weight's too much for you."

"I had him on my back for a mile getting here," Duffield said.

"Aye. But ye weren't trying to cross a rope bridge one-handed at the time."

"I said, I've got him, Sergeant," Duffield said calmly, but firmly.

"Let him try," Banks said. "What's the worst that can happen?"

"I can think of plenty."

"As it happens, so can I. But I'm tired, Wiggo. Get me home. Please?"

Wiggo turned to Duffield.

"If you lose him, you and I are going to have words," he said.

"If I lose him, I'm going to be having enough words with myself to bother with yours," Duffield replied. "But trust me. I've done fireman training. I can do this."

The high wailing and hissing got louder still. Wiggo eyed the undergrowth with trepidation.

"Get on with it then," he said. "But I won't be watching you; I'll be watching your back."

"And right glad I am of it too, Sarge. I'll shout when we're over," Duffield said, and once again hoisted the captain over his shoulder.

Wiggo couldn't watch. He kept his gaze firmly on the undergrowth, half-expecting to hear a shriek...or a pair of them... as Duffield and the Cap plunged to their doom.

No such yell came, but neither did confirmation they had made the crossing safely.

The undergrowth rustled to his right; something low and sleek was moving in there. It hissed like a snake.

An answering hiss came from his left.

Any time now would be good, guys.

-18-

Banks had a grand view of the floor of the chasm and little else as Duffield inched across the rope. He felt useless, little more than a sack of potatoes slung on the big lad's back, unable even to hold a weapon, a passive observer in every sense of the word.

Duffield was taking it slow, with none of the almost balletic grace he'd shown earlier, carefully placing his feet and checking his balance with every step. There were still live lizards on the chasm floor below, but they all appeared to be intent on feasting on their own dead, not paying any attention to the men above. There was nary a breath of wind, but the still air was now full of sound, the high, almost hissing, wails of the lizards. And as the sound grew louder, the beasts below finally raised their heads from their feeding. Almost as one they looked up, spotted the men on the ropes above, and joined their voices, loud and clear, to the cacophony. They moved towards the walls of the chasm and seconds later began to climb, coming up fast.

"Better hurry up a wee bit, lad," he said. "There's trouble coming."

He felt a lurch, as if Duffield had missed a step, but they didn't lose balance and when the lad spoke his voice was calm and steady.

"Hurrying up, yes sir," he said, and moved faster.

They were past half way but weren't going to make it in time. Turning his head, Banks saw that Wilkins and Mac were aware of the situation; Wilkins stood with the rifle pointing down into the canyon, and Mac had his pistol drawn and ready at hand. It was probably long past time to worry about giving away their position.

"Take them," Banks shouted, and Wilkins immediately complied, sending two of the beasts back down to the valley floor where the carcasses were immediately pounced on by others. Banks heard more firing, on the other side of the canyon, then felt the rope sway violently below them. He turned his head to see Wiggo, standing on the bottom rope, holding on for dear life to the other with his left hand while one-handedly pumping round after round from the rifle into a wall of lizards crowded on the far bank.

"Get a fucking move on," Wiggo shouted. "I'm coming over and I'm running low on ammo."

Duffield lurched violently, and Banks' heart flew to his mouth, the scene in front of his eyes sweeping alarmingly, so much so that he fully expected to be falling and lost, only for

Duffield to once again steady himself and begin moving again, much faster now as if throwing caution to the wind. Seconds later Banks was dumped, almost thrown, unceremoniously to the ground at the woman's feet. The dog came over and licked his face, as if checking for signs of life and Banks surprised himself by finding a laugh.

"It's okay, boy, I'll live… for a wee while longer at least."

The air filled with gunfire, and he rolled, looking up to see Duffield, Wilkins and Mac all firing back across the canyon.

"Come on, Sarge," Duffield shouted. "We've got you covered."

It only took a matter of seconds before Wiggo had joined them on the near side. All four men stood above Banks, pouring fire across the chasm, until Duffield called for a stop.

"Save it, lads. Job's done."

Banks looked across the divide. The far side was a roiling frenzy of feeding lizards and bloody carcasses. None of the beasts were now paying any attention to the men. Duffield looked down to the valley floor.

"All quiet down there too," he said. "Right, let's get on the move before they notice us again. Sarge, will you take point? I'll get the captain again."

Banks was pleased to note that Wiggo fell in line with Duffield's decision to take charge; it was one he himself was fully in agreement with, for he could think of little right then but the pain and the need to get up off the ground without immediately keeling over. Duffield again helped with that.

By the time Banks was upright and leaning heavily on both his cane and Duffield's shoulder, Wiggo was already leading the others round the chasm pathway towards the chamber that would lead them to the stairwell up and out of this damned place.

A high wail rose from the far side of the chasm as the squad departed the scene. Banks looked back. It was as if the jungle was alive back there, the fronds thrashing and swaying, boughs cracking like pistol shots as something huge came barrelling through.

"Get a shift on again, lad," he said. "Looks like Mammie's still pissed off and coming this way. She's no' going to be happy when she sees what we've done to her bairns."

-19-

Wiggo's first thought on entering the chamber was how clean it all appeared; there were no carcasses or remains, merely bloody streaks on the stone floor where meat had been dragged away. The blood was particularly apparent around the entrance to the upward stairwell, but when he stood there and looked upward he neither saw nor heard anything untoward.

"Neat wee buggers," he muttered to himself as he turned back to the chamber as the others entered. Duffield and the captain brought up the rear, and Wiggo was dismayed to see that Banks was a dead weight in the young lieutenant's arms, his eyes swirling and sunk deep in gray sockets, his cheeks hollow and ashen. The man was clearly on the verge of collapse from the pain.

"Have you got any morphine?" Wiggo asked.

"I had. It's all inside him," Duffield replied grimly. "This is as good as he's going to get."

"We need to get him out of here."

"I'm working on it," Duffield replied. "Are the stairs clear?"

Wiggo nodded.

"But the things have been doing their cleaning. That means there's still some in here somewhere."

"Well let's hope for their sakes they don't meet us; I'm in the mood to give these fuckers a right good kicking."

Wiggo grinned.

"I knew I liked you."

"That's I knew I liked you, sir," Duffield replied with a grin of his own. "You and the Corporal keep the rifles. I'm going to have my hands full with the boss here. Lead us out, Sergeant. Double time."

Banks stirred, reached into his belt and brought out two magazines.

"Looks like I'm not going to be needing these," he said. "Look after them for me."

That was all he could manage before another bout of pain hit and Banks slumped against the lieutenant.

"Like I said, Sarge," Duffield said. "Double time, if you please."

Before Wiggo got as far as turning for the stairs they heard it, the unmistakable sound of high hissing, coming from just beyond the large window overlooking the ruins of the city. Wiggo stepped over and looked out. The burned out streets below were filled with movement; lizards, hundreds of them, swarming around the mother who was just coming into view down a slope off to the left of the view. She was even larger than he'd imagined, the length of a passenger train, all sinew and muscle stretched over a jutting ribcage. As if she'd felt his gaze the great head rose and she stared right at his position. The mouth gaped and she wailed, a sound that echoed long and loud all across the old city. As one the lizards turned, like a well-drilled company of soldiers, and headed for the cliff.

Seconds later they were climbing, coming fast.

"Well, that's us fucked then," Wiggo muttered, then retreated from the window.

"Incoming," he shouted.

"How many?" Duffield asked.

"All of them, I think."

They retreated back into the doorway. Wiggo and Wilkins let the others head into the stairwell while they guarded the gap. The sound of wailing beasts was now joined by the scratch of talons on rock. They couldn't see anything out of the window from this angle; Wiggo could only imagine the scurrying, frenzied horde that were making their way up towards them.

"We should climb," Elsa said at his back. "Get well ahead of them."

"They'd catch us," Wiggo said baldly. "There's too many."

Banks spoke, barely more than a whisper.

"Leave me. Leave me a rifle and leave me. I'll buy you time. I'm just holding you back here anyway."

Both Duffield and Wiggo said the same thing at the same time.

"Fuck that."

Duffield patted Wiggo's shoulder and handed over two more magazines. "Make them count. I'll take Mac and the woman up to the next level with the Cap. Can you two hold them here for a bit?"

Wiggo nodded.

"How long do you need?"

"Two, three minutes?"

"Make it two. And if we're not with you by then, keep going up. Get them home."

"We'll get us all home," Duffield said, just as the first of the beasts showed its head over the parapet.

Wiggo put a round between its eyes and it fell away. Two more took its place.

"Good luck," Duffield said, heading up the stairs with the captain a dead weight over his shoulder.

"We'll need it," Wiggo replied, then had to focus.

Wilkins took out the latest two to show their heads, but the space was immediately filled, and more taloned hands reached for the top of the parapet as the lizards pulled themselves up.

For the first ten seconds or so Wiggo and Wilkins managed to hold their own, clearing the large window as quickly as it filled, the air filled with the crack of gunfire and the death wails of the lizards. The tide turned against them when Wiggo came up empty.

"Reloading," he called out, ejecting the mag and slamming another home. Wilkins tried to cover for him, but even a slight dip in their firepower had been enough for two of the lizards to make it almost totally over the parapet. Taking those two down gave those behind time to clamber up and now the view out of the large window was obscured by the scrambling bodies of beasts, some attempting to gain entry, others intent on feasting on the newly dead that had fallen in front of them. The stench of death filled the chamber, almost causing Wiggo to retch.

Despite a constant field of fire more and more of the lizards were now making their way over the parapet and encroached into the chamber. Wiggo could see a bad end rapidly approaching if they didn't move.

"Back up, Wilko. Into the stairwell. We'll cramp them for space. See how they like it."

Wilkins, still firing, backed up. Wiggo followed suit, staying low to keep out of the other man's line of sight. Ahead of them the lizards spilled over the parapet and started to fill the chamber even as their bodies were riddled with multiple rounds. Within seconds the two men had to retreat further as the lizards reached the bottom step.

How long has it been? Is it even a minute yet?

The only way Wiggo had to mark the passage of time was in how much ammo he was expending, and he knew that the mag was going to be running dry again in short order. Above him Wilkins ran his first mag dry and smacked in another.

They retreated slowly up the stairs, filling the stairwell with dead lizards as they went.

-20-

Banks was drifting in and out of consciousness, his mind unable to keep events in a straight narrative timeline. All he had were impressions; of bumping his head against a rock wall going up inside a narrow stairwell, of loud wailing sounds accompanied by gunfire, of white, searing pain and deep velvety blackness, all of them aswirl and existing almost simultaneously. It was as if there was a silky veil in front of his face at times, so that he could only see things dimly, but when he tried to raise a hand to part it he found that his arms wouldn't respond to commands. From the waist down all was cold, ice, stone even while his head burned with fire. At some point he became aware he was hanging over someone's shoulder like a sack of coal.

"Wiggo?" he muttered.

"No, sir. Duffield," the answer came, but he couldn't match a face with that name. He heard more gunfire, somewhere down below in the stairwell.

"Wiggo?" he said again.

"Watching our backs, sir," the answer came. "Try to keep still. It'll make this easier."

"Easier for who?" he tried to say, but no words came, just another wave of blackness, velvet, soft and free from pain. He leapt into it willingly.

When he next became aware of something he was sitting on a stone floor, his back to a wall in a wider chamber, with a dog licking his face. A woman was trying to keep the dog away from him, with little success. A burly young chap he belatedly recognized as Duffield stood beside Mac at a tall window looking out. The sound of rapid gunfire came from somewhere below, and then from closer still as both Mac and Duffield fired at something that appeared suddenly in the window frame.

"The buggers can climb, I'll give them that," Duffield said, then quickly strode back to where Banks sat.

"Off your arse, Cap," the big lad said. "Time we were moving on up. It's not safe here."

"Wiggo?"

"As I said, watching our back."

The sound of gunfire from below was getting closer, as was the high, hissing wailing. The chamber shook, as if hit by something heavy. Mac shouted from the window.

"It's the big fucker. She's coming up the cliff."

Duffield hefted Banks back up over his shoulder and shouted out.

"Everybody head up, right now."

Wiggo's voice echoed up from somewhere below.

"We're coming up."

There was another volley of gunfire from below.

The room shuddered and stones fell from the roof as the wall was hit, hard, from the outside.

There were more stones, rubble and dust falling in the stairwell as Duffield took the steps two at a time. The speed seemed vertiginous to Banks, and a wave of nausea washed over him. Rather than give in to that, he chose the blackness again.

The next time out of darkness he felt earth on his face, and almost choked as some went in his mouth and up his nose. He was still slung over Duffield's shoulders, being forced upwards almost as if the younger man was trying to put a cork back in a bottle. They were in a tight space, getting tighter. Above them someone, something, was scrambling in dirt and stone, sending runnels of both tumbling, running past Banks' head and down a flight of steep steps into darkness. From below that came muffled sounds of gunfire, tumbling rock and rhythmic pounding as if a giant hammer was being wielded. Closer by someone was swearing like a trooper, and it took Banks several seconds to realize it was him.

"I can see light," a woman's voice shouted above them.

"Nearly there," Duffield said.

"Thank fuck for that," Banks replied. "I could do with a kip."

A heavier flurry of stones and dirt fell around them, but he had enough sense to keep his mouth shut.

Duffield grunted with exertion and pushed upwards, hard. Someone grabbed Banks' arm and tugged. He popped upwards into bright sunlight and fell flat on his back on frost-hardened ground. Young Duffield pulled himself up alongside, then turned back, shouting down a hole that looked to be narrowing rapidly.

"Sarge? Corporal?"

Then, louder, more urgently.

"Sarge?"

-21-

The managed retreat turned into a rout by the time Wiggo and Wilkins reached the chamber with the window. At least the others had already made their way up, but that was the only plus point about the situation. No matter how many rounds he and Wilko had pumped down the stairwell, the lizard things just kept coming, a seemingly inexhaustible supply of them. Both men were dangerously low on ammo for the rifles, down to their last mag each. On top of that they now had what Wiggo suspected was Big Mama pounding on the wall outside, threatening to bring the stairwell down around their heads.

When they reached the window-chamber, Wiggo immediately pointed to the stairwell going up.

"Off you go, lad," he said to Wilkins. "It's a toss up whether they get us first, or the whole fucking place comes down. I say we take our chances on the stairs."

Wilkins took the lead with Wiggo following at a run. They made it up to the top chamber with little difficulty, but had only just arrived there when the pounding from below intensified and the whole place shook as if hit by an earthquake. Stone and dirt tumbled from overhead while wild scrambling could be heard from below.

Wiggo sent one last volley down the stairwell then sent Wilkins upwards into the torrent of dirt and rubble that was cascading down from above. The passageway tossed and tumbled him around as he tried to climb.

Like a fucking lost sock in a dryer.

Wilkins lost his footing above, and ended up using Wiggo's head as a stop. The passageway narrowed further, at the same time as Wiggo felt the steps beneath his feet start to give way. He could only claw upwards, using his hands like shovels, like a mole blindly digging.

He heard a muffled shout from somewhere above.

"Sarge?"

It sounded like Duffield. He didn't waste energy trying to reply, just kept digging.

"You still there, Sarge?" Wilko shouted down.

He tapped Wilko's foot and kept digging.

The passage constricted even tighter and more debris fell from above. He had little to no grip below his feet now, relying totally on arm strength to pull himself upwards, and he was tiring fast.

Then, all at once, there was light above him, and strong arms pulling at him even as the ground below tried just as hard to suck him back. With the very last of his strength he pulled himself up and out and rolled away as the hole caved in from below, widening now instead of narrowing.

He found himself in a strong hug with Elsa's arms around him and Danny excitedly jumping up at his chest.

"That was too close," Elsa said.

It was Duffield who replied.

"It's not over yet."

-22-

Banks was surprised to find that he was still gripping tightly to the rubbery cane, and surprised himself even more by using it and being able to struggle, somewhat unsteadily, to his feet, just in time to have to step back fast as the hole widened further and the huge head of the mother serpent forced its way up from below. The whole clearing rocked and rolled underfoot, almost throwing him back to the ground and bringing another wash of nausea that he had to choke down. Duffield was at his side immediately, making sure he didn't fall.

The serpent was still coming up out of the ground, its head almost totally free of the hole, but it was obviously struggling against an opposing force threatening to drag it back down into the depths.

"You got a rifle, lad?" Banks asked, dismayed at how weak his voice sounded.

Duffield shook his head, but handed Banks a handgun.

"I think the honor goes to you on this one, Cap."

Banks called Wiggo, Wilkins and Mac over to join him, and all of them took out their handguns.

"For old times' sake," Banks whispered.

All four stepped forward and put three shots each right into the serpent's left eyeball which burst like a deflating football. The beast immediately went limp, and slid, almost silently back into the hole, dragged by some huge collapse from below that took it down and away, the earth closing over it and leaving only a dug-over depression as any sign of its passing.

Danny walked over, head in the air, cocked a leg, and pissed on the dirt.

"Good boy," Duffield said.

"Very good boy," Wiggo agreed.

Danny wagged his tail in agreement.

Banks' legs gave way again, but Duffield and Wiggo held him up.

"Thanks, lads," he said, just before the darkness called for him again. "Now will one of you fuckers do an auld man a favour and take me home?"

-23-

Two weeks later Wiggo was once again called to the colonel's office; only it was no longer the colonel's office. Captain Banks' name was now the one on the office door, and Banks himself was sitting behind the big desk when Wiggo entered. Banks looked more haggard than Wiggo would like to see, but he had color in his cheeks and his eyes were clear of pain.

Lieutenant Duffield was in one of the two chairs opposite, so Wiggo took the other one.

Banks opened his arms, as if welcoming them.

"Meet the new boss. Same as the old boss," he said, and grinned. "The colonel's taken early retirement...and so, it seems, have I."

He slapped his hand against his thigh at his bad leg.

"They saved it, but it was a close thing. I'll not be doing any running from here on in though, and precious little walking if truth be told. They asked if I wanted to retire hurt, I said, *Fuck, no,* so they offered me the desk, and I said yes."

"What does this mean for the squad?" Wiggo asked.

"Well firstly, your wee off-piste jaunt didnae impress the brass very much, and that means that your promotion has been, shall we say, delayed?" Banks said. "But if you'd got it, you'd have been promoted out of the squad anyway, so I for one am happy to still have you. The lieutenant here will be your new C.O. ... I've just offered it to him, and he nearly bit my hand off saying yes. So what say you, Wiggo? Think you can help me make something of the lad here?"

Wiggo reached over and shook the lieutenant's hand.

"From one mad bastard to another, welcome aboard, sir."

CHECK OUT OTHER GREAT CRYPTID NOVELS

BIGFOOT WAR
by **Eric S. Brown**

Now a feature film from Origin Releasing. For the first time ever, all three core books of the Bigfoot War series have been collected into a single tome of Sasquatch Apocalypse horror. Remastered and reedited this book chronicles the original war between man and beast from the initial battles in Babblecreek through the apocalypse to the wastelands of a dark future world where Sasquatch reigns supreme and mankind struggles to survive. If you think you've experienced Bigfoot Horror before, think again. Bigfoot War sets the bar for the genre and will leave you praying that you never have to go into the woods again.

CRYPTID ZOO
by **Gerry Griffiths**

As a child, rare and unusual animals, especially cryptid creatures, always fascinated Carter Wilde.

Now that he's an eccentric billionaire and runs the largest conglomerate of high-tech companies all over the world, he can finally achieve his wildest dream of building the most incredible theme park ever conceived on the planet...CRYPTID ZOO.

Even though there have been apparent problems with the project, Wilde still decides to send some of his marketing employees and their families on a forced vacation to assess the theme park in preparation for Opening Day.

Nick Wells and his family are some of those chosen and are about to embark on what will become the most terror-filled weekend of their lives—praying they survive.

STEP RIGHT UP AND GET YOUR FREE PASS...

TO CRYPTID ZOO

CHECK OUT OTHER GREAT CRYPTID NOVELS

SWAMP MONSTER MASSACRE
by **Hunter Shea**

The swamp belongs to them. Humans are only prey. Deep in the overgrown swamps of Florida, where humans rarely dare to enter, lives a race of creatures long thought to be only the stuff of legend. They walk upright but are stronger, taller and more brutal than any man. And when a small boat of tourists, held captive by a fleeing criminal, accidentally kills one of the swamp dwellers' young, the creatures are filled with a terrifyingly human emotion—a merciless lust for vengeance that will paint the trees red with blood.

TERROR MOUNTAIN
by **Gerry Griffiths**

When Marcus Pike inherits his grandfather's farm and moves his family out to the country, he has no idea there's an unholy terror running rampant about the mountainous farming community. Sheriff Avery Anderson has seen the heinous carnage and the mutilated bodies. He's also seen the giant footprints left in the snow—Bigfoot tracks. Meanwhile, Cole Wagner, and his wife, Kate, are prospecting their gold claim farther up the valley, unaware of the impending dangers lurking in the woods as an early winter storm sets in. Soon the snowy countryside will run red with blood on TERROR MOUNTAIN.

CHECK OUT OTHER GREAT BIGFOOT NOVELS

THE BEASTS OF STONECLAD MOUNTAIN
by **Gerry Griffiths**

Clay Morgan is overjoyed when he is offered a place to live in a remote wilderness at the base of a notorious mountain. Locals say there are Bigfoot living high up in the dense mountainous forest. Clay is skeptic at first and thinks it's nothing more than tall tales.

But soon Clay becomes a believer when giant creatures invade his new home and snatch his baby boy, Casey.

Now, Clay and his wife, Mia, must rescue their son with the help of Clay's uncle and his dog, a journey up the foreboding mountain that will take them into an unimaginable world...straight into hell!

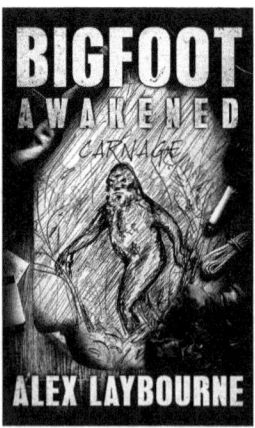

BIGFOOT AWAKENED
by **Alex Laybourne**

A weekend away with friends was supposed to be fun. One last chance for Jamie to blow off some steam before she leaves for college, but when the group make a wrong turn, fun is the last thing they find.

From the moment they pass through a small rural town they are being hunted by whatever abominations live in the woods.

Yet, as the beasts attack and the truth is revealed, they learn that despite everything, man still remains the most terrifying evil of them all.

www.ingramcontent.com/pod-product-compliance
Lightning Source LLC
Chambersburg PA
CBHW061246170626
46809CB00007B/2863